T0149236

THE MISTRESS

PREVIOUS BOOKS BY ALAN REFKIN

FICTION

Matt Moretti and Han Li Series

The Archivist
The Abductions
The Payback
The Forgotten

Mauro Bruno Detective Series

The Patriarch
The Scion
The Artifact

NONFICTION

The Wild Wild East: Lessons for Success in Business in Contemporary Capitalist China
By Alan Refkin and Daniel Borgia, PhD

Doing the China Tango: How to Dance around Common Pitfalls in Chinese Business Relationships
By Alan Refkin and Scott Cray

Conducting Business in the Land of the Dragon: What Every Businessperson Needs To Know About China
By Alan Refkin and Scott Cray

Piercing the Great Wall of Corporate China: How to Perform Forensic Due Diligence on Chinese Companies
By Alan Refkin and David Dodge

THE MISTRESS

A MAURO BRUNO DETECTIVE SERIES THRILLER

ALAN REFKIN

THE MISTRESS
A MAURO BRUNO DETECTIVE SERIES THRILLER

iUniverse books may be ordered through booksellers or by contacting:

iUniverse
1663 Liberty Drive
Bloomington, IN 47403
www.iuniverse.com
844-349-9409

ISBN: 978-1-6632-2312-8 (sc)
ISBN: 978-1-6632-2313-5 (e)

Library of Congress Control Number: 2021909984

Print information available on the last page.

iUniverse rev. date: 05/18/2021

To my wife, Kerry
To Dr. Frank Sullivan

PROLOGUE

Venice, Italy - May 1994

K ATARINA ADAMO WAS a police officer assigned to the administrative section of the Vigili Urbani, or municipal police, in Venice, Italy. She was five feet, eight inches tall, with raven black hair and dark brown eyes. The 25-year-old had an athletic body due to years of jogging, yoga, and lifting light weights. Every man on the force, married or not, had chased her but got nowhere with the stunning officer who lived by herself in an apartment near the Santa Lucia train station, within walking distance of the police station. An only child, her mother died in childbirth, and her father succumbed to a heart attack last April.

Slightly less than two years ago, she was at a bar with two of her fellow officers when she met Mauro Bruno. He was in Venice celebrating, having just graduated from college in Milan with a degree in business. He was handsome; she was attractive, and they started talking. During that conversation, she discovered his father was the chief prosecutor for the city of Milan and wanted his son to follow in his footsteps. However, the college graduate had other plans, confessing that the prospect of reading legal texts and arguing the law for the rest of his life was something that he believed would be highly boring. He, therefore, planned to look for employment opportunities that were both challenging and exciting. As the evening progressed, the conversation segued to Katarina, who gave a synopsis of her life.

"You give parking tickets?" Bruno asked, as most Italians believed this was the primary function of the Vigili Urbani.

"I work in administration. I conduct background checks on applicants who want to work in the government, contractors and their employees who require access to government facilities, and anyone else who has sustained dealings with the government."

"How do you investigate someone's background?" Bruno asked, the curiosity evident in his voice.

"I check our police databases to see if the applicant has a record, is wanted for a crime, has lawsuits or judgments against them, has known associations with criminals, and so forth. I also check Interpol's databases."

"Why don't I believe anyone can sneak something past you?" Bruno said, a comment that brought a smile to her face.

"They try. That's why I make it a point to memorize the faces and names of the Mafia family leaders and their known associates. They constantly attempt to sneak their members into a ministry."

Their conversation continued until the bar closed, and Bruno walked Katarina to her apartment, which was 15 minutes away. Following a goodnight kiss, she invited him inside.

The following day, they went for breakfast at a local café. Both acknowledged that the chemistry between them was too strong to ignore, and they impulsively decided to live together and see how things worked out. After moving in, he began looking for a job. A month later, he discovered the only positions available for someone without business experience were in tourism - a staple of the Venice economy. Katarina offered an alternative, suggesting the Polizia di Stato, the state police force, which cast a broader investigative and jurisdictional umbrella than the municipal police. Bruno never thought of himself as a police officer but agreed to look into it. The following day, she arranged for him to speak with several officers. Captivated by their experiences, he applied to the Polizia di Stato and graduated from the academy less than a year later. Shortly afterward, they married. Ten months later, Katarina was seven months pregnant.

Venice, Italy - March 23, 1996

It was 7 p.m. as Katarina and Mauro Bruno prepared to leave their apartment to have dinner before his 9 p.m. shift. As a rookie on the force, he received the least desirable patrol hours - the nine-to-five rotation. Before they left, he handed his wife a heavy piece of linen stationery, which came from a box someone gave them as a gift.

"What's this?"

"It's a fraction of the reasons I love you. I'm grateful you came into my life, that we're about to have a baby, and that our child will have the most wonderful mother in the world."

"I love you too. You're the only person with whom I could spend my life. I want to read this letter when I return home. I don't want to rush through it," she said before kissing him.

They were both in uniform as they ate at their favorite restaurant, Trattoria alle lance, which was close to their apartment. Katarina didn't return home to change beforehand because the owner expressed his gratitude to law enforcement by giving anyone in uniform a ten percent discount. Therefore, whenever they ate at the trattoria, they avoided civilian clothing.

The dining portion of the restaurant was unevenly divided into two - the main area and a semi-private alcove with a rectangular table that could seat six. Mauro, who faced the alcove, rubbernecked to see who sat there.

"What are you looking at?" Katarina asked, seeing him gazing over her left shoulder.

"I want to see if anyone in the alcove brought his mistress or niece. It doesn't look like it."

Katarina smiled. Both learned in casual conversation with the restaurant owner that those who were having extramarital liaisons favored this intimate and private area. Katarina turned around and caught the stare of one of the four men. Her expression instantly changed from curiosity to deep concern. She refocused on her husband.

"What is it?"

"I recognize three of the four men at that table."

"Who are they?"

"Armino Acconci, Baldassare Pagano, and Romelo Ricci."

Bruno shook his head slightly, indicating that he was unfamiliar with those names.

"Acconci is the Mafia don for the Venice-Padua-Trieste area, and Ricci is his enforcer. Pagano is the don for the area in and around Rome. Acconci and Pagano are the heads of two of the five families on the commission: the Mafia's governing body. At least that's what our intelligence briefs show. What is Pagano doing here, and who is next to him? I thought I knew all the top players in the Mafia."

"You can write this up when you get to your office in the morning. Until then, go home so that you and the baby can get some sleep." He signaled the server for the check. After receiving it, he put cash on the table and helped his wife out of her chair. Once outside the restaurant, they kissed and went their separate ways.

As Mauro Bruno held up his hand for the bill, Acconci asked a passing server if they knew the couple in uniform.

"Signore e Signora Bruno," the server replied. "They live close, so they're regulars." Although he usually wouldn't have answered the question because the restaurant respected a customer's privacy, the server knew the identity of the person who'd asked and wasn't about to turn down his request.

Once the server departed, Acconci looked at Pagano. "What do you want to do?"

"Kill the woman," he replied without hesitation.

Pagano was five feet, five inches tall, and 46-years-old. Newly installed as the commission's chairperson, he exercised significant influence over the other four families since he had the final say on matters affecting the Mafia in Italy.

"I could see from her expression that she recognized me," Pagano continued. "If she investigates why I'm in Venice, her curiosity could lead to exposing Riva. I can't let that happen. Even though he's a relatively unknown politician, that will change. It was a mistake to sit down with him in public."

The three mafiosos and Riva came to the restaurant from Acconci's estate, which was just outside the city proper, where Riva updated the commission on his progress in climbing the ladder to the top spot within the government and what impediments needed to be eliminated for that to happen. He gave this progress report once a year so that each family could provide their input. The four were at this restaurant because Pagano and Riva were waiting for the next train to Rome, which didn't leave for three hours, and Acconci and Ricci wanted to make sure there were no issues with their departure. Acconci had suggested they pass the time by having dinner, believing that the locals wouldn't know Riva. On that, he was correct.

Ricci got up from the table, needing no further direction. The 24-year-old native of Trieste was six feet, two inches tall, with close-cropped black hair and a prominent nose that looked to have been broken at least once. He had wide-set dark brown eyes and large callused hands that were as coarse as sandpaper.

Following Katarina Bruno, he kept his distance as she walked down a sidewalk in front of retail shops that closed two hours earlier. Thankfully, the pregnant woman wasn't setting any speed records. This allowed him to maintain a casual pace and not arouse suspicion as he kept her in sight. Spotting two pedestrians ahead, he buttoned his jacket so that the silenced weapon under it wouldn't be visible, and patiently waited for them to pass.

The street they were on had three distinct sections. It began with restaurants, gradually transitioned to retail stores, and finally to residential apartments. Once the two pedestrians were some distance away, he lengthened his stride to close on his target. He was about to unbutton his jacket, withdraw his gun, and give the woman a quick double-tap when a man walked out the door of a business and turned in his direction. Ricci put his hand by his side. As the man passed, Katarina Bruno opened the door to her apartment building - which was the first one in the residential section of the street.

When Acconci and Pagano caught up with Ricci, he was standing outside the building. They had no trouble following because they saw through the restaurant window that the enforcer turned right as he left and, since that street had no intersecting roads for over a quarter of a mile, they didn't lose him.

"The woman's inside. I saw that light go on," Ricci said, pointing to the corner apartment on the third floor.

"Get us inside," Pagano ordered.

Ricci removed a leather pouch from his pocket and got to work. A minute later, he'd picked the front door lock.

Quietly making their way up the interior stairwell to the third floor, the three men went to the corner unit where Ricci had seen the lights go on. After he picked the lock, they entered with their weapons drawn. However, only Ricci's had a suppressor.

When they heard a noise coming from the bedroom, Ricci took the lead, with Pagano and Acconci following. Katarina was standing next to the dresser removing her jewelry and had her back to the door. On her head were lightweight headphones connected to a Sony Walkman. Without delay, Pagano took Ricci's weapon and put a round into the back of her head.

"We need to make this look like a robbery," Pagano said, picking up the spent shell casing off the floor before handing the weapon back to the enforcer. "Grab a pillowcase and throw whatever might be of value inside."

They began ransacking the apartment. Ricci unplugged the laptop on the desk in the living room and put it and the power cord inside the pillowcase, along with whatever else was on or inside the desk. Since they only needed to create the illusion of a robbery and wanted to leave the apartment as quickly as possible, he didn't look at what he was stealing. Acconci and Pagano worked the bedroom and took the jewelry that Katarina had removed, the small jewelry box on the dresser, and whatever else they thought had value. Fifteen minutes after entering, they left unobserved.

Mauro Bruno discovered his wife's body when he returned home at 5:30 a.m. Collapsing on the floor in grief, he held her in his arms for 20 minutes before reporting what had happened. Although the police listed the incident as a robbery-homicide, no one could explain why the thief picked this apartment over the others, especially the penthouses on the top floor. They also couldn't explain why they murdered a pregnant woman who, although a police officer, was unarmed.

Initially, detectives pursued the investigation with the vigor and enthusiasm that one might expect from such a heinous crime against one of their own. However, with no leads, the case eventually regressed from red hot to a cold case file on someone's desk. Bruno, who became a chief inspector and a legend within the Polizia di Stato, had only one investigative failure in his storied career - finding his wife's murderer. Although he was recused from the formal investigation, he worked the case in secret and came up with nothing - an open sore that tormented him in the succeeding years.

CHAPTER 1

Rome, Italy - June 15, 2010, 11:30 p.m.

GRATIANO RIVA WAS a rising political star, progressing from an obscure bureaucrat to a ministerial-level position thanks to being sponsored by senior members of his party. The impetus behind this sponsorship was a combination of bribes and threats by the commission.

Riva was popular with the people thanks to a constant flow of favorable articles and social media releases by a PR firm that received payment for their services from an offshore corporation. His wife, Gabrielle, was plain - being neither attractive nor unattractive. She was five feet, one inch tall, 32-years-old, and thin with virtually no breasts. Her 39-years-old husband, however, had gotten more handsome with age. He was six feet, three inches tall, on the thin side, and had light gray eyes and jet-black hair. His teeth were white and in perfect contrast to the tan, which he maintained year-round thanks to a nearby tanning salon.

Those who saw the couple found it unfathomable that he could pass up the multitude of beauties who threw themselves at him, many of whom came from wealthy families, to marry someone who was the opposite of eye candy. However, no one knew that Pagano picked who he would marry and when the union would occur. The caveat in this matrimonial arrangement was that he didn't exclude his rising star from liaisons - and Riva had many of them before getting married because he was a womanizer.

Publicly, there was speculation about whether he currently had dalliances and, if he did, if his wife knew about them. The betting line was that someone as handsome as Riva had indiscretions and that his wife knew about them and turned a blind eye to his affairs because of his increasing importance within the republic and the lifestyle it afforded her. These rumors failed to gain a foothold and, over time, appeared to be contradicted by the image of a devoted family man who went to church on Sundays and held his wife's hand when they were in public.

The Rivas had no children, Pagano forbidding it because it would take a significant amount of time away from building his career. His wife, Gabriele, went along with that decision because she didn't consider herself the least bit maternal and wanted a life free of the encumbrances of raising a family. The only thing that could change her mind would be an opinion poll which showed her husband was unlikely to continue his political rise without progeny.

Pagano was a control freak regarding Gratiano Riva. He hired professional speechwriters and funded numerous opinion polls that gave what the public liked and disliked about his protege. He also bought wardrobes for him and his wife that gave them a good look for the social circles they were entering, selected her engagement and wedding rings, and purchased their residence in the right neighborhood.

Knowing Riva was incapable of not having an affair and that the public's scrutiny of him would only increase, Pagano told him to settle down and get a mistress. The only restrictions placed on that relationship were that he couldn't embarrass his wife or tarnish his image by taking her out in public or discussing family business or personal matters with her. She was strictly for sex - the venues for which Pagano limited to after-hour trysts at one of Riva's two offices or his mistress's apartment.

Over the years, Riva had several mistresses, who kept their silence because of Pagano. He met his latest at a government party given by Pia Lamberti, then the wife of the president of the republic, who introduced them. The woman was stunning. Standing five feet, nine inches tall, she had dark brown eyes and shiny raven black hair that gently caressed her shoulders. Her proud breasts were large, well-shaped, and perfectly suited to her tight body. Following the introduction, Riva had the singular focus of talking her into being his latest mistress. For two weeks, he lavished her with gifts and attention, eventually sealing the deal after handing her the key to a penthouse apartment that Pagano agreed to let her use.

Riva was the Minister of Infrastructure and Transport, ascending to that post after the previous minister drowned while swimming in Sardinia. Today, he worked from the Quirinal, his liaison workspace down the hall from the president's office. Although he spent most of his time at the ministry building, he enjoyed conducting business from here because it was near the seat of power to which he aspired.

His mistress was waiting for him to finish up so they could have a quickie, after which she'd return to her penthouse - a customary sequence when he worked late at the liaison office. Leaving a private restroom, she walked down the short hall leading to the discrete rear entrance to Riva's office.

Even in the dim lighting, she looked stunning in a Missoni chevron knit wrap dress and Gucci Palmyra Leather Platform Espadrille Wedges, which elevated her height to an even six feet tall. The antique red agate cameo sterling ring, which she usually wore on her right hand, was in a discrete pocket in her dress, forgotten there once she had washed her hands. As she neared her lover's office, she heard him speaking to Pagano. The walls were thin, and she was curious what they were saying because they never talked about anything of substance when she was around. Placing her ear to the door, she listened to their conversation. The two seemed in conflict, the dispute centering on Riva's wife and someone named Vespa. As she adjusted her weight, there was a creak. The conversation immediately ceased.

Riva was speaking when he and Pagano heard the creak. Familiar with the Quirinal, they understood it could only have been caused by someone standing on the old flooring, which meant they were listening to their conversation.

Creaks were common in the Quirinal, a building constructed over half a millennium ago. Because the building had shifted over time and damaged the floor joists, this resulted in sections of the flooring sagging - rubbing together and producing a creak when someone stood on it or shifted their weight. The Quirinal was currently undergoing a massive restoration, beginning with the president's office, and proceeding down the hall towards the liaison offices. So far, they hadn't gotten to Riva's. Therefore, he still had the old flooring.

"My mistress," Riva mouthed to Pagano.

"I can't take the chance. I have to assume she overheard us. I'm sorry, Gratiano, I'll take care of it." Pagano said this in a whisper.

He made two calls in quick succession, speaking in a voice so low that even Riva couldn't hear. When he'd finished, he put his phone inside his jacket pocket, went to the rear door, and opened it. As expected, the mistress was standing there.

"Baldassare," she said, extending her hand, which the Mafia leader gently took and kissed. "It's nice to see you again."

"I didn't know you were here."

"I was freshening up."

Pagano said that he'd heard a noise and wanted to see what it was. "It must be the pains of an old building," he said as he extended his arm and escorted her into the office. The three carried on a casual conversation for nearly 30 minutes, after which Pagano said that he was going to his car and offered to walk her out of the building if she was ready to leave.

"I'll see you tomorrow," Riva told his mistress, ending any thought of her remaining. "Baldassare will take you home." Kissing her on the lips longer than usual, he gently ran his hand down the left side of her cheek.

Knowing she had no choice but to leave, the mistress took Pagano's arm, which he'd extended.

They left Riva's office and turned right, toward the VIP security station in the center of the 1,000,000-square-foot-plus building. This route took them past President Orsini's office where, before the Quirinal's renovation, there was a 24/7 guard posted outside his door. However, since the president was occupying a temporary office at the opposite end of the building, security shifted to that location.

"Have you ever seen the president's office?" Pagano asked as they approached.

"No."

"Then let me show you," he said, entering the access code into the keypad.

"The president gave you his entry code?"

"I own the construction company performing the restoration. The project supervisor, foreperson, and several others know it so they can let the workers inside. I'm sure they'll change the code once the restoration of the office is complete."

Pagano opened the double doors and turned on several LED construction lights, after which he closed the entry doors. The wooden floors, the president's desk at the rear of the office, and the rectangular conference table to the right as one entered were covered with clear plastic sheeting. The restoration of the office appeared to be nearly complete because the president's personal items, such as framed pictures and desk accessories, could be seen under the sheeting.

"It's beautiful," the mistress said, looking at the intricate woodwork and gilt throughout the office. "Where does that door lead?" she asked, pointing to the rear of the office.

"The president's private bathroom and shower. I've never been able to figure out if that chandelier is Murano. Perhaps you have a better eye," Pagano said as he changed the subject and pointed to the majestic fixture above them. Once she looked up, he moved to the side.

The knife that cut her throat began at the left ear and, in a descending arc, continued to her right, after which she fell to the floor and bled out on the plastic sheeting. The murder weapon was the president's letter opener, taken by the killer from under the plastic covering his desk. It was a birthday gift from his wife, who was tired of him constantly complaining that his current letter opener was so dull that it tore rather than cut. His wife gave him a knife, honed so sharp that it slit a piece of hair, to replace that opener. Although the president and his wife referred to it as a letter opener - it was a knife.

Pagano picked up the letter opener off the floor with his handkerchief and placed it next to the body. Removing the cell phone from his pocket, he called Attilio Sanna, a second-generation mafioso who worked for his construction firm. The thug was waiting inside his car just outside the Quirinal because of the call from Pagano. He entered the palace using his construction pass and went to the president's office. When he entered, his eyes focused on the tightly wrapped plastic bundle.

"Cut a hole in the wall beside the body and hide it inside. Then patch and sand it smooth," Pagano ordered. "I want no unevenness because the wall's going to be papered."

"It'll be as smooth as a baby's behind," Sanna promised. "But if you like, I can bury the body outside the city where no one will ever find it."

"Everything leaving the palace goes through an x-ray machine," Pagano reminded him. "Besides, it'll be half a century or longer before the next restoration of this office. By that time, the body will be mummified."

Although Pagano's logic was sound, he couldn't have foreseen that a decade later, Antonio Conti, an alias for the terrorist Ammar Nadeem, would attempt to destroy the Quirinal. In the process, the shock waves produced by an explosion caused significant damage to the interior walls, thereby speeding up Pagano's predicted timeframe.

CHAPTER 2

Present day

T HE DETECTIVE AGENCY was called BD&D Investigations, named for its three partners - Mauro Bruno, Elia Donati, and Lisette Donais. It listed two offices on its business cards - one in Milan and the other in Paris. While that looked impressive to prospective clients, the address in Paris was Donais's apartment, and their office in Milan was a four-bedroom apartment with a large rectangular conference table that served as their communal desk. On the second floor of a white five-story historic building in the Corso Di Porta Romana neighborhood, the 2,800 square foot space was a few steps from the Duomo.

Three months ago, they prevented the destruction of the Quirinal, the principal residence of the president of Italy in Rome. They also saved the lives of three heads of state, one of whom was the president of the United States, along with a considerable number of diplomats. In the process, the three investigators learned that someone was transporting a dirty bomb towards the White House. Informing US intelligence, a Secret Service sniper killed that person seconds before he was to detonate it. Although no one outside of a few knew of their heroics, BD&D Investigations had considerable investigative credibility and political clout in Italy and the United States.

Bruno was sitting at the communal desk, opening the mail that he'd retrieved from their postal box in the lobby. Most were advertisements, which he discarded into the trash bin beside him. That dwindled the stack to two letters addressed to him. Opening one, he saw another client referral from Dante Acardi - his third in as many months. Although the assignments weren't complex, they brought revenue to the fledging firm along with name exposure. The second letter was a white envelope with no return address. The canceled postage stamp affixed to it showed it came from Venice. Bruno opened it. Inside was a single piece of heavy linen stationary, which was at odds with the envelope's cheapness.

The stationary seemed familiar, although he couldn't put his finger on the reason. Unfolding the letter, he quickly realized why. He was holding the letter that he'd written and handed to his late wife before they left their apartment for dinner on March 23, 1996 - the night that she and their unborn son were murdered. Stuck to the bottom of the letter was a yellow Post-it note. Written on it in black ink with a heavy hand was an email address and, below that, a message: "I know who killed your wife and unborn child." Bruno stared at the letter in shock.

"What is it?" Donati asked. Donais looked equally concerned.

"Read the yellow note," Bruno responded in an uneven voice, handing the letter to Donati, who was sitting to his right. Donais, who was on the other side of Bruno, got up from her chair and looked over Donati's shoulder.

"Is this real?" Donais asked once she read it.

"I wrote that letter to my late wife the night someone killed her. They took it in the robbery."

"And 20 years later, someone sends it to you. Why?" Donati asked.

"Twenty-five years," Bruno corrected. "It seems the answer to that question will only come when I acknowledge receipt of the letter to that email address."

"You never told us the circumstances of your late wife's death. If you're up to it...," Donais said, her voice trailing off.

Bruno told them.

"You have no clue who did it?" Donais asked.

"They recused me from the investigation for obvious reasons. The robbery itself made no sense. We were poor. Our apartment, which was in a less than middle-class neighborhood, was on the third floor of a four-story building, and we were the only unit robbed."

Donais, tears flowing down her face, gently put a hand on Bruno's shoulder.

"And no one heard the gunshot?" Donati asked.

"No. That led the investigating officers to believe the killer used a silencer."

"And the shell casing?"

"Was never found. The killer probably picked it up before they left."

"No gunshot. No casing. It sounds like a professional hit."

"That's my belief. The detectives assigned to the case were the best we had. They worked tirelessly trying to find the killer. In the end, they came up empty. Eventually, priorities shifted, and the case became a cold file."

"Are you going to email whoever sent this?" Donais asked.

"After I take a photo of the note and text it to Acardi. I need his help to get a copy of my wife's case file and access to the Polizia di Stato's database."

Bruno was referring to Dante Acardi, the deputy commissioner of the state police who lived in Rome and who Bruno and Donati indirectly reported to when they were chief inspectors.

"What will you do if you find the killer but can't prove they're guilty because the evidence won't hold up in a court of law?" Donati asked.

"If I'm positive they did it, they're never going to trial. I'll give them the same consideration they gave my wife and unborn child."

"Which is?" Donati asked although the tone of his question showed he already knew the answer.

"None."

Dante Acardi's flight from Rome arrived at Milan's Malpensa airport at 8:30 a.m. the following morning. He entered the offices of BD&D Investigations an hour later. Just as with his last visit, he arrived unannounced. At that time, Donais didn't know the identity of the person who barged into their apartment/office and came close to putting a bullet into him before Bruno made the introduction. This time, the stunning five feet, four inches tall blonde, who had a spectacular torso and the legs of a model, gave him a warm hug. That brought a broad smile to the face of the 63-year-old sexagenarian. While this was happening, Donati went into the kitchen and made the deputy commissioner a cup of espresso, bringing it to him at the firm's communal desk where he'd taken a seat. Bruno was at the head of the table;

Donais was to his left, and Donati to the right. Unsurprisingly, Acardi sat next to Donais.

"Grazie," Acardi said, taking a sip of espresso.

"You came to see the note," Bruno said, assuming the purpose of the visit.

"I want to take the original Post-it note back to Rome for lab analysis. Forensics has gotten much more sophisticated in the two-and-a-half decades since the murder. Perhaps the sender touched or licked the stamp, and we can extract a DNA sample. As you know, we have an extensive DNA database."

"I'd appreciate that," Bruno said.

"May I see it?"

Bruno retrieved the letter with the attached Post-it note, which he'd placed in a letter-size plastic sleeve, a habit formed from decades as a police detective. He handed the sleeve to Acardi.

"I touched the envelope, but not the note."

"Your fingerprints are on file, so we can eliminate them."

Acardi read the letter, letting out a sigh at the end. He then looked closely at the note through the plastic sleeve before placing it inside his black leather briefcase, which he habitually carried with him.

"Did you email this person?"

"I asked our techs to look into this email account. Whoever sent this note took great pains to remain anonymous. They're using a Swiss service provider with an international reputation for fastidiously protecting their client's identities. They take pride in denying government requests for information on their users."

"There must be a reason they reached out to me after such a long time. They want something. The question is: what?"

"What do you need from me beyond the lab analysis?"

"The old case file and access to your database."

"You'll have it. Let me know if there's anything else." Shifting his weight slightly in his chair, Acardi gave the trio a sheepish look as he cleared his throat. "I know this is an awkward time to bring this up, but I need your help on a very sensitive matter."

The three investigators were silent, but their expressions reflected suspicion because the deputy commander of the state police wanted their help even though he had tens of thousands of officers working for him. The last time he'd asked for it, they were almost killed.

Without waiting for a response, Acardi opened his briefcase and removed a folder. He placed it on the conference room table and slid it towards Bruno.

"I have a body with no name, and I need to find the killer."

"Which is what the Polizia di Stato does," Bruno replied. "Come on, Dante. Why go outside for investigative help? What aren't you telling us?" Bruno asked.

"That he doesn't trust those working for him to keep whatever he's going to tell us a secret," Donais said.

"That's correct."

"Then this visit wasn't just about seeing the note," Donati interjected.

"Initially, it was. However, after I received your text, something came up."

Acardi took a sip of espresso before continuing.

"Let me explain. The terrorist explosion outside the Quirinal, while causing some structural damage, produced cracks in the walls throughout the presidential palace," Acardi said, referring to the underground natural gas explosion perpetrated by Islamic terrorists who tried to ignite the gas they'd pumped beneath the palace hoping to kill scores of

NATO dignitaries and several heads of state. While the three investigators prevented that from occurring, a pocket of gas ignited outside the palace. The resulting explosion shook an area a mile in diameter and collapsed a street on the north side of the Quirinal.

Bruno opened the folder. Inside was a series of photos, which he spread in front of him. Donati and Donais left their chairs and stood behind their partner to get a better view.

"The photos to your left show the damage the explosion caused within President Orsini's office."

The investigators saw a jagged three-inch-wide crack extending from floor to ceiling in the wall beside the president's desk.

"This doesn't look like much," Donati said.

"It isn't. The Quirinal's director of engineering, Eriberto DeRosa, believed one of the palace's maintenance and engineering staff could repair it in less than a day."

"And then it got interesting," Bruno added as he looked at the other photos.

"An understatement. The president decided that he would work for the day from another office at the opposite end of the palace during the repairs. He left one of his security guards to watch the maintenance person, who began by taking a saber saw and cutting out the damaged portion of that wall. When he removed it and looked within, his light shone on a desiccated body wrapped in thick sheets of plastic. I'm told the elderly gentleman almost had a heart attack."

Acardi explained that when the guard who watched the worker saw the body, he called President Orsini, who then phoned DeRosa. Both came immediately to the president's office. "Wondering what else was hidden behind the wall, the president ordered it to be completely exposed. However, nothing else was discovered inside."

"This knife?" Donais asked, tapping a photo.

"Is the murder weapon. It was inside the plastic sheathing encasing the victim."

"You said you don't know the identity of the victim," Bruno said, repeating what Acardi noted earlier.

"All we know is that she was in her 20s when she died. Facial recognition and fingerprint searches, both in Italy and with Interpol, came back negative."

"This wasn't in the news," Donati said.

"Six people, excluding yourselves, know about this - myself, the guard, the worker, the director of engineering, the president, and the coroner. He's holding the body under the name Jane Doe."

"Was she stabbed?" Donati asked.

"Her throat was cut."

"Any luck in tracing the murder weapon?"

"It was a letter opener used by former president Gianluca Lamberti. He reported it missing while in office. This isn't going to help his legacy."

"A young woman found dead behind the wall in his office, with the knife he used as a letter opener as the murder weapon. No, Dante, this isn't going to help the late Gianluca Lamberti's legacy."

"Hence, the discretion of having the three of you investigate."

"Did the coroner establish a timeframe for her death?"

"She died approximately ten years ago. Coincidentally, that was the last time the president's office underwent renovation."

"Does the Quirinal keep a detailed record of who enters and leaves the palace?" Donais asked. "If so, our suspect is probably on that list."

"I have the entry and exit registers going back a decade. Excluding daily visitors and the construction workers involved in the renovation, an average of 1,720 employees worked at the palace."

"How many had access to the president's office?" Donais asked.

"Twenty. However, the entry code was given to the construction company. Who knows how many of their workers went in and out of that office on any day?"

"We'll need to speak with the coroner and get a copy of his report on Jane Doe," Bruno said.

"I'll make both happen."

"Being suspicious by nature, our investigation wouldn't also have something to do with the upcoming election?" Bruno asked.

"It has everything to do with it. The Polizia di Stato, like all government agencies, leaks information like a sieve. You know that. Since this is an election year, an investigation will quickly become a significant distraction from the record of achievements on which the president is running. The election is close. His challenger, Gratiano Riva, is constantly attacking him on issues he knows the president has no control of, but the public doesn't. Riva is young, energetic, and appealing to young voters."

"I obviously know who Riva is," Bruno said.

While Donati also said that he was familiar with Riva, Donais was silent. The native Parisian was new to Italy and not familiar with Italian politics or the upcoming election.

Acardi, knowing Donais knew nothing about Riva, looked at her as he continued. "Some feel it's time for a younger generation to take the reins of government. Even though this murder occurred during the last presidency, it could convince a majority of voters that a change in leadership is needed. Unless we find the killer quickly, what I told you will eventually get out, and the opposition will spin it to their advantage."

"As much as I'd like to help, I don't have the time to investigate this murder. My priority is finding my wife's killer. For the first time in 25 years, I have a lead. This may be my only chance to get closure on a sore that still hasn't healed. Elia and Lisette can take the assignment. I'm out."

"I understand. If I were you, I'd make the same decision. However, this is important for the country, Mauro. Otherwise, I wouldn't be here." Acardi took a deep breath, seemed to be lost in thought for a few seconds, and then looked Bruno in the eye. "Maybe, there's a way for both of us to get what we want. How about this? You interface with whomever is on the other end of that email address while your partners investigate this murder. I'll give you the cold case file on your wife's murder and provide whatever data you want. In return, you work on the investigation as time permits. The time you devote is strictly up to you. I need your investigative instincts - not to take anything away from your partners."

"We understand," Donati said, getting an approving nod from Donais. "No offense taken."

Bruno thought for a moment before responding to Acardi. "That's fair, Dante. If that arrangement works for my partners, it works for me."

Donati and Donais said they had no problem with it.

"I haven't got time now to give you more details because time is short. I'll tell everyone on the flight to Rome."

"What flight?" Bruno asked.

"What details?" Donati asked almost immediately afterward.

Acardi removed three airline tickets from his bag and handed them out. "These are open tickets on the commuter flight to Rome. The next one leaves," he said, looking at his watch, "in an hour. If you pack quickly, we can just make it. I'll call ahead and have the cold case file available for you when we arrive in Rome."

"You were pretty sure of yourself," Bruno replied.

"I was sure that the three of you wouldn't let a guilty party go free."

CHAPTER 3

"**W**HEN WILL YOU respond to his email?" Ricci asked Pagano.

"I haven't decided. His reputation indicates that he's astute. Therefore, I'm going to bring his emotions into play. That should make him careless, more vulnerable, and easier to kill."

Ricci formerly worked for another Mafia don, Armino Acconci, and then for his son, Lazzaro. The son's tenure on the commission ended abruptly when a business transaction that he got the families into cratered. Pagano had him killed and gave another family the Mafia's territorial governance for northern Italy. With that change, he brought Ricci to Tivoli as his lieutenant.

"The law of unintended consequences," Pagano added, staring in the distance.

"Sir?"

"Actions sometimes have unintended or unanticipated effects. In this situation, not killing Bruno along with his wife resulted, decades later, in the collapse of Rizzo's empire and the loss of an invaluable service that he provided the commission."

Ricci nodded as if he understood, but the confusion in his eyes indicated otherwise.

Pagano's interest in killing Mauro Bruno wasn't because he feared that Bruno was looking for him and would put a bullet in his head for killing his wife. If Bruno knew he was responsible, he'd have had him arrested or attempted to kill him decades ago. Instead, killing Bruno was an act of revenge because he drove Duke Rodolfo Rizzo to commit suicide. The duke was the founder and chair of the Bank of Rizzo, Italy's largest financial institution, which laundered most of the illicit cash for the five families comprising the commission. With his death and the exposure of the bank's illegal activities, their ability to launder money came to an abrupt halt. Having to reestablish this function made it significantly more expensive and time-consuming to wash their cash. Pagano, who didn't become chairperson of the commission by having the word forgiveness in his lexicon, was exacting his revenge on the former chief inspector.

Before going after Bruno, he wanted to learn all he could about him. After hiring an investigative agency in Rome, he obtained copies of the cases Bruno solved during his career, background before joining the Polizia di Stato, and his habits, biases, and other inclinations. This provided him with a keen insight into how the former chief inspector made his deductions and reacted to adverse situations. Once wholly familiar with his adversary, he sent the letter and attached Post-it note.

As Ricci was about to leave Pagano's study, Attilio Sanna knocked on the door and was given permission to enter. "The recorder from Signor Riva," he said, handing it to Pagano.

Ricci and Saana left the room without being asked, knowing that their boss always listened to the daily recording by himself.

The procedure for passing information from Riva to Pagano was simplistic. Gratiano Riva had been the Minister of Infrastructure and Transport for more than a decade. During this time, he always took a taxi to and from his office despite being offered a ministry vehicle, driver, and security detail. He did this over the protestations of government security officers, concerned that the head of a significant ministry and a candidate for president was in constant danger of being harmed, killed, or kidnapped by some whack job. Local citizens, however, had a different point of view. They saw a young minister who believed that he was one of them.

However, no one knew that the taxis that brought him to and from work and anywhere else he wanted to go belonged to the commission's chairperson, who rotated five of his most trusted men to transport Riva. A digital recorder would be on the taxi's rear seat, and Riva would record whatever he needed to say. If he wanted to leave copies of papers or other sensitive material, he would remove those from his briefcase and place them on the back seat. As Pagano owned two taxi companies in Rome and one in Tivoli, a different vehicle was used to transport Riva daily. This way, in the unlikely event anyone compared license plates, no pattern would be detected. In addition, the drivers were indiscernible because of the tinted windows.

Pagano connected his headphones to the recorder and pressed play.

My ministry received a call from one of the maintenance supervisors in the Quirinal requesting a no-bid contract to replace the entire wall to the right of the president's desk, which he said was cut open and removed for a visual inspection. We, therefore, have a problem. He didn't mention a body, but it's improbable that they did not discover her and that she's now at the old morgue pending identification. None of my sources at the state police know anything about this. However, one told me that their deputy commissioner was called by the president and flew to Milan the following morning to meet with BD&D Investigations. You need to make this go away for both our sakes.

The recording ended.

Pagano summoned his sounding board, Romelo Ricci, back to his study.

"The body of Riva's mistress has been discovered," Pagano said. "And, with the law of unintended consequences in full force, the state police may be using Bruno and his associates to investigate the murder to keep it quiet."

Pagano cleared his throat, placed his fingers in a steeple in front of his lips, and thought for a full minute before returning his gaze to Ricci.

"If we do this right, we can use the discovery to benefit Riva and give him a political bludgeon against Orsini, even though the murder predated his term of office."

"How?"

"It's obvious that Orsini, Acardi, and a handful of others are keeping the discovery of the body a secret. Otherwise, one of our government informants would have told us about it. We need to make that discovery public while ensuring it and the autopsy report go missing, and the coroner is killed to add to the mystery. This will make it look like the president has something to hide. He'll spend the last months of his campaign playing defense. The election will belong to Riva."

"You want me to steal the body and the autopsy report and then kill the coroner?"

"Yes. But don't kill him until he erases the report from his computer system and the backups. I also want you to kill the investigators from Milan, as they've undoubtedly been told too much."

"Respectfully, won't all these deaths raise questions?" Ricci asked.

"Combine those with the death of the coroner and the missing body and autopsy report, and the nation will demand answers to something Orsini is incapable of explaining. He'll spend his time trying to stay above water and take his focus off the campaign."

"If you want to Kill Bruno yourself, I could bring him here after I kill the others."

"As much as I would enjoy it, I don't have time. Nor do I have the time to continue my email charade with him. I need to take advantage of the opportunity that just presented itself."

"What do you want to do with Acardi? He knows more than anyone."

"I'll decide how to kill him later. His death needs to be separate and apart from the others."

"Do you know when the investigators will arrive in Rome?"

"They may already be here. Assuming they aren't, have our men watch the Ciampino and Fiumicino airports and the train stations. Get their photos off the internet and text them to each of our men. If someone sees them, they're to follow and call you. You take it from there."

As Pagano was giving his instructions to Ricci - Bruno, Donati, Donais, and Acardi arrived at the Ciampino airport. On the flight, Acardi told them the details he'd previously excluded - which was that the mummified woman was well-dressed yet wasn't wearing jewelry.

"That indicates that she wasn't homeless. You'd think someone would have reported her missing," Donati, who sat in the narrow economy class seat to the left of Acardi, said.

"Because she wasn't wearing jewelry, robbery could be the motive for her murder," Acardi volunteered.

Donati said that was a possibility, but it would be difficult to determine if anything was stolen without knowing the deceased's name.

Acardi agreed.

Bruno, who sat to the right of the deputy commissioner while Donais had the aisle seat across from him, noticed a tenseness in Acardi's voice - which was unusual. He also saw that he touched his neck, a vulnerable part of the body, was very still and stared - classical signs that he was being less than forthright. If he were still a chief inspector and the deputy commissioner was his suspect, he would believe that Acardi was holding something back. The question was: what?

With no checked luggage, they went straight to Acardi's unmarked government vehicle - a black Fiat 500X subcompact SUV parked in one of the law enforcement slots outside the main terminal. As they were walking, Acardi began receiving texts, his expression indicating that he wasn't thrilled by what he read. Putting his cell phone in his pocket, he opened the tailgate on his vehicle.

"Don't take these inside the presidential palace," Acardi said, handing Bruno and Donati holstered Glock 17's and four clips of ammo. "Ms. Donais, this should be small enough to fit in the handbag you brought with you," he said, handing her a Glock 17 without a holster and two clips.

"Should we rent a car?" Bruno asked.

"Use mine," the deputy commissioner replied, tossing the keys to Bruno. "There are additional gun magazines and weaponry in the rear. I assume you'll want to start your investigation at the Quirinal."

Bruno said that was his intent.

"I'll arrange for you to see the president and Eriberto DeRosa. While you're doing that, I'll be putting out some fires at the office."

"We can drop you off."

"I'll take a taxi. It's in the opposite direction of the palace. Just keep me in the loop," Acardi said as he walked towards the taxi stand, which was less than 25 yards away.

The three investigators drove to the Quirinal. Acardi called ahead, and the security station issued each an unrestricted pass, which gave them access to the entire palace. When they went to President Orsini's office, which they'd been to before, and Bruno knocked on the door, Eriberto DeRosa opened it and invited the investigators inside. The trio's eyes were involuntarily drawn to the large opening in the wall, failing to see the president sitting behind his desk.

"It makes you wonder what else is hidden within this million square foot building," President Orsini said as he stood, approached the investigators, and shook each of their hands. Since they knew each other, introductions weren't necessary.

"The coroner believes the body was behind this wall for around ten years," Bruno said.

"That sounds about right," DeRosa responded. "There was a restoration of this office in 2010. There would be no way to get a body behind this wall unless that type of work was occurring. Once the restoration was complete, access to this office was restricted, and a guard, such as the one you saw outside, was posted beside the door."

"Is this office soundproof?" Donais asked.

"We have special rooms for those types of conversations. My office isn't one of them," the president answered.

"How do you ensure someone didn't hide a camera or listening device during the construction?" Donati asked.

"Once the contractor completes their work, a special unit from the military sweeps the office for traces of explosive materials, biological agents, clandestine electronics, and anything else that's not supposed to be here. Periodically and unannounced, they'll perform the same checks," DeRosa answered.

"Yet the military never x-rayed behind the walls, or they would have discovered the body," Bruno said.

"A failing I'll rectify once this matter is over," President Orsini said.

"Whoever did this had to know the renovation schedule and have the access code," Donais said. "As far as we know, the contractor was the only one who had both."

"Who was the contractor?" Donati asked.

"Heritage Restorations," DeRosa said.

"By definition, that makes them our prime suspect until the facts dictate otherwise," Bruno said. "What do you know about them?"

"They're a top-notch company that delivers what they promise."

"Did they get a non-bid contract for this renovation?" Donati asked."

"Non-bids are only for minor repairs. Large companies like Heritage don't go after those contracts because their overhead is too high, and they'll lose money," DeRosa answered.

"How did they get the restoration contract?"

"The Ministry of Infrastructure and Transport issues construction and renovation contracts."

"Who's the largest restoration contractor?" Donais asked.

"Heritage. Ninety percent of their business comes from the government. That's fine with me. They do flawless work done and finish on time. I've never had an issue with them."

"Who owns Heritage Restorations?" Bruno asked.

"Sebastiano Piras is their CEO. I don't know if he's the owner, but I believe he is."

Following a few more questions, the trio said they had everything they needed to get started. Leaving the president's office, DeRosa took them to one of the engineering conference rooms.

"Use this room as your office while you're here," DeRosa said. "Let me know if there's anything you need."

When Bruno answered, they were fine for the moment; DeRosa gave him his cell number and office extension before leaving.

As Donais and Donati removed the laptops from their carry-on's, Bruno called Acardi, who answered on the third ring.

"Can we meet with Sebastiano Piras at Heritage Restorations?"

"When?"

"Now. We also need to see the coroner."

"When?"

"At the end of the day."

"I'll arrange both. Don't tell Piras about the body."

"I didn't plan to."

"Just a reminder."

"What are you going to say when he asks why he's meeting with three private investigators? He'll ask," Bruno said.

Acardi thought for a moment before answering. "You're independently reviewing the security protocols used when outside contractors work in a government building," Acardi volunteered. "Since he's the largest contractor, you want his input."

"That sounds believable," Bruno said.

"Try not to interrogate Piras. I don't want him to become suspicious. Approach him as gently as if you were walking on glass barefoot."

"You know us, Dante. At one time, Elia and I worked for you."

"Which is why I bought a large bottle of Maalox tablets at a pharmacy near my office. Hopefully, I have enough."

CHAPTER 4

ONCE ACARDI CALLED and confirmed the meeting with Piras, the three investigators got directions from DeRosa to the headquarters of Heritage Restorations, which was in EUR, an abbreviation for Esposizione Universale Roma. Although it was only seven miles from the presidential palace, it would take them 30-minutes in regular Rome traffic to get there.

The planning for EUR began in 1936, intending to expand it towards the south and west so that it would eventually become the center of Rome. To advertise this development, Benito Mussolini proclaimed it to be the site of the 1942 world's fair, which would celebrate Italy's 20 years of fascism. World War II interfered with those plans, and the exhibition never took place. Once the war ended, the area's tenants became corporations and government ministries and agencies, which discovered that EUR's extensive garden and park-like settings reduced stress among its employees and significantly increased productivity.

Heritage Restorations' headquarters was a series of five single-story buildings, each approximately 5,000 square feet. The architecture was mid-century modern, with perimeter offices having sliding-glass doors that led to outside patios, each with a small wrought iron table and two matching chairs. A forest of trees, thick grass, and lush shrubbery surrounded the complex. Zigzagging through the area were concrete walking paths and biking lanes. Parking was kept out of sight and below ground so as not to disturb the aesthetics.

Bruno parked his vehicle, and the three investigators followed the signs to the elevator - which took them to the lobby. After giving the receptionist their names and presenting photo IDs, they were told that Mr. Piras was expecting them and to sign the guest log. They did and were issued visitor's badges and given directions to his office. Five minutes later, they were standing in front of a middle-aged woman sitting behind a glass desk supported by two aluminum pedestals. Following a cursory greeting, she got up, knocked on the door to her left, and opened it without waiting for a response.

Piras's office was large and rectangular, stretching across the width of the building. The right and left sides each had three sets of sliding glass doors which led to enormous patios. The interior was uncluttered and functional. At the rear of the office was a glass desk, slightly larger than the one used by the middle-aged woman, behind which was a forest green leather chair. No other chairs were near it. A laptop sat in the middle of the desk.

To the right, as one entered, was a large rectangular glass conference table supported by six aluminum pedestals. There were eight Herman Miller Aeron chairs on either side, plus one at each end. The walls displayed the many awards the company won, but there were no photos or memorabilia anywhere within the office. Piras was at the conference table, standing over a set of blueprints. Once the trio were inside, his assistant left and closed the door behind her. The CEO came forward, and the parties introduced themselves and exchanged business cards.

Piras was six feet, one inch tall, with thick arms and a torso carrying an extra 30 pounds of weight. The 56-year-old had gray hair and sun-damaged skin, which was wrinkled and dry, making him look ten years older. He took a seat at the head of the table and motioned for the trio to sit.

"The deputy commissioner told me why you're here. What would you like from me?"

"Exactly what he said. A description of the security protocols your company uses when your employees work in government buildings."

Piras gave them a detailed description of how his company kept security tight on a project, ensuring that only their employees were on-site and that the many valuables they worked around weren't permanently borrowed by one of them. He also detailed the background checks they performed on applicants before submitting them for approval to the Vigili Urbani.

"Impressive," Bruno admitted. "We'd like to inspect your record keeping."

"The deputy commissioner failed to mention that. The term record-keeping is vague and covers a lot of territories. Can you be more specific?"

"I want a list of every employee who worked on the renovation of the Quirinal in 2010," Bruno replied. "I want to see how much time each spent in the building and which rooms they worked in."

"That's very specific."

"As you requested."

"Can I ask why you want to look at records from a decade ago?"

"The Quirinal renovation was a large contract performed over a significant period. If your record-keeping was good then, we'll assume you maintained the same level of integrity to the present day."

The look of disbelief on Piras's face indicated he wasn't buying it.

"That information will be difficult to provide."

"Why? You're required to keep records of work performed on all government contracts ad infinitum," Donati interjected.

"I know my responsibilities," Piras testily responded. "We have the records that document our work. However, unlike other restoration companies, our employees are not paid hourly. They receive a salary. Therefore, they work as long as it takes and wherever they're needed to get the job done. Also, the government contracts on which we bid are fixed-price and not hourly. There's no requirement to provide how many hours each employee works or where they're used. The government only cares that the work for which they've contracted is done on time and to their satisfaction."

"You're saying that, internally, there's no way to tell where an individual worked within a project nor how long they were there?"

"That's what I'm saying. Employees go wherever their supervisor tells them."

"Your system seems to work because Eriberto DeRosa told us your restorations are flawless and that you complete your projects on time," Bruno interjected.

"He's easy to work with," Piras said.

"What did you do before Heritage Restorations?" Bruno asked.

"I owned a small restoration company in Tivoli."

"And you moved it here?"

"I sold it and started this."

"And you only take projects in Rome?"

"I have no geographic restrictions."

"Whoever bought your Tivoli company must have overlooked you signing a non-compete agreement. Are they still in business?"

"No."

"You've built an impressive company. These buildings, the land, your labor pool, and the materials for the projects must have required a substantial amount of up-front capital for you to start this business. Did you do this by yourself or do you have partners?" Bruno asked.

"By myself. The money to start this business came from the money I received for selling my company and from bank loans, which I've since repaid. That information is in the application I filed to become a government contractor."

"Impressive. Getting back to why we're here, can I get a list of every employee who worked on the Quirinal restoration?" Bruno asked.

"Certainly. Where should I email it?"

After Bruno told him, the trio stood, again shook hands with Piras, and left his office.

Once in their vehicle, Donati was the first to speak. "What do you think?" he asked, throwing the question up for grabs.

"He's smooth," Donais replied. "He's also smart enough to know we're looking at something which occurred during his renovation of the Quirinal."

"What do you think?" Donais asked Bruno.

"That we were speaking with the wrong person," Bruno said.

Upon returning to the Quirinal, the three investigators went to DeRosa's office and found the engineer sitting at his desk.

"Find anything?" DeRosa asked.

"We're getting traction," Bruno said. "A question. Who is Heritage Restorations' largest competitor?"

"Restoration Associates. Although Heritage wins most of the government contracts, Restoration Associates cleans their clock in the civilian market."

"Interesting. Would it be possible to have their CEO come here and speak with us?"

"I'll ask. The same premise?"

Bruno nodded.

DeRosa called Pasquale Gentile, the company's founder, chairperson, and CEO. An hour later, he was ushered into the conference room that the trio was using as their office. Once introductions were made, everyone took a seat at the circular table.

"I was told that the purpose of this meeting was that you're reviewing the security procedures used by contractors working in a government facility."

"That's correct," Bruno confirmed.

"You should expand your review beyond security and inspect Heritage Restorations. They're crooks."

"Why do you say that?" Donati asked with a surprised look, mirroring DeRosa, Donais, and Bruno's faces.

"Because they win most of the government contracts issued by the Ministry of Infrastructure and Transport. No one's that good or lucky."

"My understanding is that companies submit a sealed bid. The low bidder receives the contract," DeRosa said.

"If you do the math, you'll discover that no company can have their entire workforce on salary and bid lower than a workforce of hourly employees. It's impossible given the benefits the law requires employers to attach to those who are salaried."

"They must make money," Donais replied. "As the saying goes, you can't make up a loss with volume - meaning a greater number of projects. As you said, do the math."

"They don't make money on the basic contract. They lose money on it."

Bruno asked him to explain.

"They make their money on addendums to the contract, which we in the industry refer to as change orders. When Heritage wins a bid, there's always one or more change orders attached to the basic contract. They're very profitable because no one is bidding against you and your crew is already on the job. You give a price for the work requested with the ministry being the only determinator as to the fairness of that quote."

"You can play the same game," Donati said.

"I can't. My company never receives a change order. If I played that game, I'd be bankrupt. Therefore, I must submit a realistic bid on the basic contract. That makes me the high bidder."

"You've won government contracts," Bruno said.

"Window dressing so as not to arouse suspicion that they rigged the game."

"You're saying someone wants Heritage to receive most of the contracts."

"You're damn right I am."

"What do you know about Sebastiano Piras, the owner of Heritage Restorations?"

"Piras isn't the owner. Everyone in the business knows it's Baldassare Pagano."

"Pagano?" Donais asked.

"The head of the Mafia in Rome," Gentile replied.

"You're saying the Mafia controls the bidding process at the Ministry of Infrastructure and Transport to exclude, on most bids, anyone but Heritage Restorations and that they only give change orders to Heritage contracts? Those are serious accusations. Why don't you lodge a complaint with the government?" Donais continued.

"Because I, and anyone else who files a complaint, will be dead before we can testify."

With the subject of employee security protocols forgotten, and having gotten more than they bargained for from Gentile, they thanked him for his time, and DeRosa escorted him out of the room.

"It's obvious why Piras says that he's the owner of Heritage," Donais said. "I don't think the ministry could get away with awarding a government contract to a business owned by a Mafia don."

"Something's also going on with the issuance of change orders, or they wouldn't be so lopsided," Donati said. "It seems likely that the Minister of Infrastructure and Transport is in the middle of this."

"His subordinates could have kept him in the dark," Donais said.

"Possibly, but that would be a hard sham for anyone to maintain for over a decade. If Riva is as smart and energetic as people say, he's not someone that lets a subordinate handle large contracts that, if mismanaged, could come back and bite him," Donati added.

"I agree," Bruno said. "However, none of what we heard gives us any indication who was in the president's office when Jane Doe was murdered, why she was killed, or who she is."

"What's next?" Donais asked.

"We visit the coroner, examine the body, and see if we can figure out this woman's identity. Acardi felt her clothing and lack of jewelry were important. We'll look into those. Let me call and see if he arranged the meeting," Bruno said.

Donati and Donais were talking when Bruno ended his call.

"The coroner is expecting us at 7:30 p.m., which is an hour and a half from now," Bruno said.

Donati and Donais were both smiling.

"What's with the smiles?" Bruno asked.

"Lisette and I were saying that this is the first case we've worked where no one is shooting at us. We could get used to this."

"We've been in Rome less than a day. I wouldn't exactly call that a trend," Bruno replied. "We could still dodge a bullet or two before the end of the day."

His prediction was a gross understatement.

CHAPTER 5

THE FIAT'S NAVIGATION system informed Bruno that they'd arrived at the address Acardi gave them. Stopping the SUV next to the call box at the entrance to the morgue parking lot, he pressed the red button and gave his name. Moments later, the security arm raised. Bruno drove into the lot, which was empty except for one vehicle in the row of spaces closest to the rear of the building, and pulled into a space.

As they were getting out of the vehicle, a man exited the rear entrance. He was five feet, nine inches tall and around 60 years of age. He had gray hair combed straight back, a muscular build, and a thick neck - both of which seemed to show that he frequently exercised with weights.

"I'm Ernesto Labriola, the coroner," the man said. Extending his arm, he shook hands with his three visitors.

After the trio introduced themselves, Labriola punched a code into the keypad beside the door and led them into the building.

Two men, sitting across the street in a white Opel Corsa, watched as the three investigators followed the coroner into the morgue, which was on a side street in an older commercial area where businesses had closed for the day. They were the advance team sent by Ricci to scout the area for any sign of trouble before the team's arrival.

"Call," the driver said to the man beside him.

The man phoned Ricci, informing him that the three people whose photos he texted them were there and inside the morgue.

"This couldn't have worked out better. We're on our way," he said before the phone went silent.

After relaying to the driver what he was told, the men reclined their seats, lit a cigarette, and waited for Ricci and the team to arrive.

The coroner led the three investigators through a maze of corridors to his office, which was at the opposite end of the building. On his desk was a large brown paper bag, and beside it a police evidence bag containing a blood-encrusted knife.

"The victim's clothing is inside the bag. The knife is the murder weapon, which the deputy commissioner sent over," Labriola said.

"Do you have any idea who she is?" Bruno asked.

"No. The deputy commissioner ran her fingerprints and the computer-generated reconstruction of her face that I gave him through every database he could access. All came back negative."

"Then you know what she looked like," Donais said, with a note of surprise.

"I do," Labriola replied, removing from his desk a five-by-seven-inch color image of the victim produced by the reconstruction software. He handed it to Donais while Bruno and Donati looked at it over her shoulder. Once the investigators memorized the face, Donais put the picture in her purse.

42

"She was stunningly beautiful. It wouldn't be easy to forget a face like that," Bruno said. "If we circulate this picture, someone will eventually recognize her. It's difficult to believe she's not in the EU database since all citizens of EU member countries are required to have a national ID card. The facial recognition software should have identified her."

"Unless she isn't from the EU," Donati volunteered.

"She'd need a passport to enter the country. Immigration would have scanned and stored the photo from her passport when she presented it for inspection," Bruno said, recalling what he knew from over two decades of law enforcement experience.

"How many times have you been unable to eventually identify a Jane or John Doe when you had a picture of their face and fingerprints?" Donati asked Labriola.

"It's a process that sometimes takes time, given that the deceased may not be from the EU. The police circulate their photo to hotels, look at missing person reports, check with immigration, and so on. Most of the time, the deceased is identified."

"How many times didn't that happen?" Donati pressed.

"Four - all under mysterious circumstances."

The three investigators looked quizzically at him, waiting for the coroner to fill in the blanks. Eventually, he got the hint and explained.

"Each time, two men came to see me regarding a John or Jane Doe. They presented a photo ID from a government agency, which I later googled and discovered didn't exist. They asked to view the body and, after seeing it, demanded every scrap of paper regarding them. They also told me to destroy all computer data on the deceased."

"And you did what they said?"

"You would, too. Their suit jackets were unbuttoned, and I could see their weapons."

"Keep going," Bruno said.

"They took the autopsy report and the notes that I made, then watched as I erased the computer data from both my primary and backup hard drives."

"What happened to the bodies?" Donais asked.

"They took them. When I opened the rear door to let them out, I saw that their vehicle had government plates. If you ask me, they were from one of the intelligence agencies."

"That's an avenue I hadn't considered," Bruno confessed. "And you were the only one who saw them?"

"I always lock up. They must have known I'd be by myself."

"How would they find out about a John or Jane Doe?" Donati asked.

"When the morgue receives a body, we take photos and post them to an online file we create for the individual. Eventually, that file contains the results of the autopsy, toxicology, and so forth. Some government agencies and ministries have access to the coroner's network."

"Did you do that for Jane Doe?" Bruno asked.

"No, I was told by the deputy commissioner not to follow that procedure."

"If some government agencies and ministries have access to your system, then why would they need you to delete information?" Donais asked. "They can do it themselves."

"Their access is read-only. They can't change, delete, or add a file."

"I'm curious," Donati said. "What happens with a body that needs to go to the morgue after you lock up for the day?"

"This isn't the only morgue in Rome. The body is brought to one of the other facilities. They're larger and newer than this and operate 24/7."

"Yet, as the head coroner for the city of Rome, you work from here," Donati continued.

"I've worked in this building for 32 years. It feels like home. If I need to perform an autopsy at another morgue, I go there. Otherwise, I can review lab results, look at a body, and so forth on my office computer."

"That means the other morgues may have received one or more house calls from the two individuals who visited you."

"Possibly."

"Why wasn't Jane Doe taken to one of the other morgues?"

"I've known Dante for over two decades. He called, and I volunteered to help. This morgue is smaller and, therefore, easier to hide a body because there's fewer prying eyes."

"Getting back to your visitors," Bruno said. "Did they say anything before they left?"

"Each time they told me they were never here, and the body they took never existed. They also said that if I had a memory lapse, I'd end up on one of my tables."

"Yet you told us."

"Don't let me regret it."

"Mind if I have a look at the contents of the paper bag?" Donais asked, changing the subject. "I want to look at the clothes."

"Go ahead."

Taking the bag to a small rectangular table at the back of his office, she removed the contents and placed them on the table. Inside was a Missoni chevron knit wrap dress with an extensive amount of caked blood on the upper half, which cracked as it dried. She carefully unfolded the dress and laid it out. Also inside the bag was a pair of Gucci Palmyra Leather Platform Espadrille Wedges.

"No undergarments?" she asked Labriola from across the room.

"No."

"Anything with a Missoni label isn't cheap," Donais, who was a fashionista, said.

"How much do you think her dress cost?" Bruno asked.

"Approximately €1,500."

Bruno's eyes widened, not familiar with the cost of designer clothing.

"How about the shoes?"

"I tried on a similar pair. The cost is reasonable - around €750."

Bruno shook his head. "Acardi must have known how expensive the clothing was when he mentioned it to us on the plane. Since few can afford to dress like this, it might provide a clue to her identity."

"The lack of jewelry is troubling," Donais said. "Given the expensive dress she was wearing, you would expect that she would wear jewelry."

Donati took the clear plastic evidence bag containing the knife off Labriola's desk. He saw traces of blood along its sharp edges.

"Can we take the murder weapon and clothes with us?" Bruno asked.

"If you sign for them, they're yours. The deputy commissioner told me I should regard the three of you as members of the state police."

As Labriola filled out the form for Bruno to sign, Donais returned the shoes to the bag and began refolding the dress, careful to avoid the caked blood. As she did, she felt something hard. Looking closely at that spot, she discovered a hidden pocket. Reaching inside, she removed an antique sterling ring with a red agate cameo on top. As no one saw Donais's discovery, she quickly put the ring on the index finger of her right hand and turned it so that the cameo was facing her palm. She then placed the dress back in the bag.

"That should do it," Bruno said as he handed the signed form to Labriola.

"Follow me," the coroner replied after putting the form on his desk. "I'll take you to Jane Doe."

As Labriola was escorting the three investigators to the refrigerated coolers where the bodies were stored, a windowless black van pulled behind the Opel. Ricci stepped out and approached the two men in the Opel. Each had an AK-47 beside them.

"Stay here and call me if there's any trouble. If you see any of the three investigators leave the building, kill them. If it's anyone else, hold them until I arrive."

Both men said they understood.

When Ricci returned to the van, six men were standing beside it. "Let's do this," he said, leading the way towards the back door.

Ricci always wore Doc Martens slip-resistant steel toe boots for both their comfort and ruggedness. Twenty years ago, he would have examined the lock on the door in front of him and patiently picked it. However, as he got older, his patience deteriorated, and he no longer wanted to take the time to pick a lock. Instead, he preferred planting the heel of his Doc Martens boot into the deadbolt and splintering the door frame. Since most frames were relatively thin and constructed from softwood, he found this was a faster means of entry.

However, after examining the frame surrounding the rear door, he found it was metal. Not bringing his lock picks with him, he sent one of his men to the van to retrieve a crowbar. When he returned, Ricci placed the flattened end between the door and the frame. Using the curved end as a fulcrum to provide leverage, he pulled until the deadbolt gave way with a loud pop. Although no alarm went off, the sound of the metal crowbar bending the frame, followed by the deadbolt breaking free, wasn't exactly quiet.

"Kill the three investigators and anyone else you find, but not the coroner," Ricci said. "I need him to give me the autopsy report and erase it from the primary and backup hard drives. Once that's done, bring the woman's body to the van and wait for me. Understood?"

When the six men said they did, everyone withdrew their gun from their shoulder holster and entered the building.

The morgue was an older building whose interior was reconfigured so often that its corridors resembled a maze if looked at from above. Although the office floors were carpeted, the hall floors weren't. They were concrete, which had the adverse effect of amplifying footsteps, conversations, and other noise - carrying those sounds throughout the building.

"The knife entered the throat in a descending arc, the killer standing behind the victim," Labriola said, explaining the slit across Jane Doe's neck as he presented his findings to the trio.

"What does that tell you about the murderer?" Donais asked.

He was about to answer when the scraping of metal, followed by a loud metallic popping sound, echoed down the halls of the building. "What is that?" Labriola asked.

"Unless I'm mistaken, someone just broke into the rear of the building," Bruno answered. "I don't know what they're after, but we're not sticking around and find out. Is there another way out of the building other than that entrance?"

"The lobby."

"Lead the way," Bruno said in an urgent voice as he removed his gun from the shoulder holster.

Donati did the same.

Donais, taking the Glock 17 from her purse, racked the slide on her weapon and picked up the brown paper bag she'd placed on the floor while viewing the body.

Labriola had just pushed the stainless-steel rack containing Jane Doe back into the refrigerated roll-in cooler when Donais, seeing the shadows of two men with handguns in the open doorway, lunged at him.

"Everyone down," Donais screamed as she tackled the coroner onto the floor. Less than a second later, a round sailed over her head. Those from the second shooter hit the refrigerated cooler behind Bruno. He and Donati dove to the floor following Donais's warning and had their guns aimed at their assailants.

Bruno was the first to return fire, with a two-round burst. Donati shot a hair later. Each put two bullets into the heart of their target, both of whom were standing in the doorway. Labriola, seeing what happened, froze with fear, quaking like a leaf on the floor.

"Unless you want to be on a slab next to them, you need to get us out of the building," Bruno said, as Donais helped the coroner to his feet.

The coroner started towards the door.

"Good instincts, Lisette. You and Labriola lead the way. Elia and I will watch your backs."

Unfortunately, they only made it 15 feet before one of Ricci's men rounded the corner from a perpendicular corridor in front of them. Running at full speed, he collided with Donais. Being outweighed by over 100 pounds, she glanced off him and slammed into the wall. The man, barely affected by the impact, regained his balance and raised his gun. In contrast, Donais's weapon was pointed at the floor, and there wasn't enough time to get a shot off before the man pulled the trigger. That never happened. Instead, her would-be executioner's head jerked sharply to the left, and he collapsed onto the floor with a circular wound visible above his ear. Donati, who was following Donais, had put a bullet in him.

"Let's go; we need to get to the lobby," Donais told the coroner, who was looking at the dead man.

Following Labriola, they went down a series of hallways. "How much farther to the lobby?" Bruno asked as they entered a hall that was longer than the others.

"Through the double doors ahead and on the right," he answered, still shaking with fear. "They're hard to see from here because they're flush with the wall."

No sooner had the coroner gotten those words out of his mouth than a gunman appeared behind them. Bruno and Donati, who brought up the rear, didn't see or hear him. They were focused on what was ahead and didn't hear his approach with the noise they were making. Donais did when she turned towards Labriola. As she raised her gun to kill him before he could get off a shot, she didn't see two of Ricci's men at the end of the corridor, which was 30 yards behind her. Bruno and Donati were looking in that direction. What followed was the trio simultaneously yelling for everyone to "get down."

As everyone hit the floor, bullets from both sides of the hall flew over them.

If one wanted to split hairs, the good news was that they were low to the ground and not an easy target. The bad was that they were in a corridor with assailants on both sides who would eventually adjust their aim and kill them.

Bruno removed the phone from his pocket and called Acardi, who heard the gunfire and quickly got the point of the call.

"Acardi is sending help," Bruno yelled over the sound of the gunfire as he returned the phone to his pocket.

"How long?" Labriola asked.

"He didn't say. My guess is too long. If we want to live, it's up to us," Bruno said, as a bullet grazed his jacket and a series of others hit the floor inches away from the four, peppering them with splinters of concrete.

While Pagano's men were relatively good shots, they were not marksmen. They were thugs who carried guns. They didn't go to the shooting range because they didn't need to. Most of their kills were point-blank. Bruno and Donati spent decades on the police force, and both qualified as expert marksmen able to hit a target at a distance that Pagano's men could only dream of. Donais, although a private investigator before becoming a partner in the firm, put in a substantial amount of time on the range and could hold her own with her partners.

"You take the one on the right, and I'll take the one on the left," Bruno said. Both understood, without saying it, that the only way to kill the persons shooting at them from this distance, given they had a handgun, was to stand and get into a stable shooting stance - which wasn't the prone position. Standing in unison and ignoring the bullets that were so close they could feel the rush of air as they flew by, they quickly assumed an isosceles stance. With their arms fully extended, their feet shoulder-width apart, and the gun in the middle of their chest, they each fired once. Both put a round into the center mass of their target.

Donais was focused on the person behind them. When he stopped shooting, she saw he ejected his magazine and was reloading. As he did, she stood, adjusted her aim, and put two into him.

"We got this group," Bruno said, looking over her right shoulder. "But there may be others. Let's get out of here."

As the four entered the lobby, they looked out the glass doors at the commercial businesses across the street.

"We need to get into one of those shops. It'll be easier to defend ourselves from there until Acardi's team arrives. I'm thinking the shop directly across the street with the brick wall below the window."

"That's a good protective barrier," Donati conceded.

"Better than the wooden frontages on the other buildings," Donais added. "That wouldn't stop a round from an air rifle."

With everyone in agreement on where they were going, the four streaked across the street and into a print shop that advertised digital offset printing on its rectangular storefront window. Although the door was locked, Donati put his shoulder into it and splintered the wooden frame. As the door flew open, bullets struck the building, shattering the storefront window. Everyone took cover behind the brick wall.

"So much for wondering if we killed everyone who's after us," Donais said.

"Did you see where the shots came from?" Bruno asked her. She raised her head. "Two perps are standing in the street beside a white Opel," she responded. "It looks like they have AK-47's."

The perps fired another barrage, and Donais lowered her head. Her partners returned fire and saw the gunmen retreat behind their vehicle.

"We don't have enough ammunition to withstand an assault," Donati said. "They have as much in one clip as we have in all of our magazines combined. At least it won't take long to transport us to the morgue," he quipped.

The look on the coroner's face indicated he didn't appreciate Donati's levity.

"Put Labriola behind the printing press," Bruno told Donais, pointing to the PressTek Offset Printing Press, a seven-ton-plus beast that was slightly over thirteen feet long, ten feet wide, and five feet high. "We'll use it as our fallback position."

Donais took Labriola behind the giant machine.

"What's holding up Acardi?" Bruno asked. As he pressed send, the two perps sent another hail of bullets into the store. Donati returned fire.

"I'm out," Donati said, the action on his weapon open. "They've worked their way to within 15 feet of us. Our next exchange is going to be up close and personal."

Acardi came on the line. "Dante, we're across the street from the morgue at a printing shop getting our asses kicked. If your team takes any longer, you can tell them to skip coming here and stop by the morgue and pick up four body bags."

"The team leader says they're almost there."

"Tell him to put *they almost survived* on our tombstones," Bruno said, breaking off the call.

53

Donais slid her handgun across the room to Donati. "You're a better shot," she said. "There's one in the mag and one in the chamber."

"Thanks, Lisette. Stay down. It's going to get wild."

"How many rounds do you have?" Donati asked Bruno.

"Four in the mag and one in the chamber," he answered, after releasing his clip and checking. "Seven rounds total. Let's make them count."

Bruno and Donati took cover behind the printing press. Figuring the two gunmen had to pass the space where the window had once been, they pointed their weapons at the opening. They weren't disappointed. However, the outcome wasn't what they expected. The two men with AK-47's ran in front of the window, pointed their automatic weapons inside the print shop, and let loose with a fusillade of bullets. Bruno and Donati never got off a shot.

CHAPTER 6

"IT AMAZES ME that someone is always trying to kill the three of you," Acardi said, sitting with Bruno, Donati, and Donais in the bar of the Marriott Grand Hotel Flora. "You've been shot at more in the short time you've been private investigators than I have in my 30 years on the force."

"In all fairness, I should mention that much of the assault on our lives have been because of the assignments you've given us. This time, we almost didn't make it. If the quick response team hadn't arrived when they did, you'd be identifying us in the morgue," Bruno said.

"I heard a very expensive printing press had something to do with your survival."

"It saved our lives, although the proprietor of that shop would probably have chosen the machine's survival over ours."

"The coroner was pretty shaken," Acardi said.

"You can't blame him - bullets were flying in every direction. It was intense," Donais responded.

"Do you know who attacked us?" Donati asked.

"You mean, in the two hours since we rescued you? No," Acardi answered in a manner that suggested Donati should get a grip on reality. "I did, however, recognize one of those you killed. He hung out with Baldassare Pagano's lieutenant, Romelo Ricci."

"Which means Pagano's after us," Bruno said.

"It looks that way."

"If he is," Donati added, "I would assume it's because of our visit to Piras."

"A good assumption. Exposing Heritage Restorations would eliminate the company from competing for government contracts and cost him a great deal of money. Changing the subject, I'm curious if the person who sent you the Post-it note replied to your email," Acardi said, looking at Bruno.

When Bruno said they didn't, and looking despondent after his reply, Acardi gave his friend a pat on the shoulder as he got up to leave.

Once Acardi left, everyone agreed to meet for breakfast at eight. Low on energy after the adrenalin rush from the gunfight, the three investigators left the bar and headed for their rooms to get some rest. While Bruno and Donati went straight to bed, Donais stayed awake, having two issues that were bugging her. One was finding the manufacturer of the ring she still wore on her index finger. Hopefully, that would lead her to the seller and subsequently to the buyer. All of this assumed that the manufacturer was still in business and kept detailed records for at least the last decade because there was no way of knowing when the woman purchased or received the ring. If it was mass-produced and widely distributed, that complicated everything.

The other issue Donais wanted to get out of the way before going to bed was to find a list of the shops and boutiques in Rome which sold Missoni dresses. Since the brand was very expensive, she believed there weren't many stores in Rome which carried it-assuming Jane Doe purchased the dress in Rome.

Getting started, she opened her laptop and searched for the manufacturer of the ring. She did this by looking for similar ones, which she hoped to trace to the designer, manufacturer, and distributor. However, by 2:15 a.m., she failed to find a single ring that even vaguely resembled the one she wore on her finger.

Donais was fading fast and decided she needed a large caffeine intake if she wanted to stay awake. Going to the coffee maker above the minibar, she inserted an Illy Dark Roast K-Cup pod and brewed herself a cup of gourmet coffee. With the influx of caffeine, she got a second wind.

Deciding an alternative approach was warranted, she wrote on the piece of paper in front of her what she knew about Jane Doe. First, she was attractive. Second, her dress and shoes were expensive. Third, since her clothing was expensive, she would assume the ring was as well. Jane Doe had all the markings of someone in high society or associated with those who were. If that was true, she probably attended one of the many charity affairs thrown by the upper crust, photos of which routinely appeared in the society section of magazines and on social media.

Running with this reasoning, she searched for high society events during the presidency of Gianluca Lamberti, who died four months ago of a heart attack, placing the picture of Jane Doe that Labriola gave her next to the computer keyboard. However, after an hour of looking at high society functions in Rome, she hit a dead end. She wasn't in any of the photos. If she attended, Donais was certain a photographer couldn't resist taking and publishing a picture of the stunning woman.

It was 3:30 a.m., and she needed a few hours of sleep before meeting her partners at eight. She went into the bathroom, and before removing her makeup, took the ring off her finger. As she did, she felt a slight movement in the cameo. Using the MagniLight app on her cell phone, she turned the brightness to maximum and zoomed in on the edge of the cameo. There was an almost undetectable gap beneath it. Putting the tip of her fingernail into it, she lifted the cameo. Underneath was a tiny headshot photo of Pia Lamberti, the wife of the late president, and a face she'd seen many times in the society pictures that she'd just looked at.

"Holy mother of God. What other hiding places did you have?" Donais said to herself as she grabbed one espadrille and twisted and pulled at the platform. Nothing moved. However, when she tried the other shoe, the bottom turned to the side, revealing a cavity. Filled with excitement and anticipation, she turned the shoe upside down, and something fell out. Holding it in her palm, her expression reflected disbelief at what she saw.

"What happened?" Pagano asked, seeing Ricci's dour expression.

His lieutenant looked at his feet, saying that he failed to retrieve anything from the morgue and that he was the only survivor.

"How were you so lucky?"

"I didn't chase the investigators. I searched the refrigeration trays for the woman's body and looked in the coroner's file cabinets and computer system for the autopsy report."

"Did you find her?"

"She's listed as Jane Doe."

"And the autopsy report?"

"It's not in the computer system, nor the file cabinets in the coroner's office."

"But you retrieved the body?"

"I wanted to take it to the van, but by the time I returned from the coroner's office to get her, the police were arriving in force. I abandoned the van and walked until I could get a taxi. I barely escaped. I can go back to the morgue, wait for the police to leave, and get the body," he volunteered.

"Too risky. Law enforcement will have extra patrols in the area and increased security at the morgue."

"Was the van ours?" Pagano asked, continuing his rapid-fire questioning.

"I stole it earlier in the day."

How many men did I lose?"

"Eight."

"And they couldn't kill three private investigators?" Pagano asked in disbelief.

"They're very good."

"That's comforting."

"Nothing links you to the attack."

"Except the bodies of my men. The police will take their fingerprints, identify them, pull their rap sheets, speak with snitches, and eventually conclude I'm their employer."

"Do you want to lay low for a while and give the investigators a pass?"

"The opposite. The longer they remain alive, the more opportunity they have to identify the woman and connect her to Riva."

Pagano took a Davidoff Madison 515 cigar from the humidor on his desk, cut off the end, and lit it with a solid gold Dupont quadrille lighter. After several puffs, he returned his gaze to Ricci. "Here's what you need to do," he said, explaining his plan.

Mauro Bruno was sound asleep when Donais pressed the doorbell for his room, the piercing sound causing him to sit bolt upright in bed. Bruno, who preferred to sleep in his underwear and a t-shirt, turned on the master switch next to the bed. Every light in the room went on. Going to the door and looking through the peephole, he saw Donais. "Just a second," he said before going to the chair over which he'd draped his pants. After putting them on, he opened the door.

"It's ... three-thirty," Bruno said, having turned around to look at the clock on the nightstand.

Donais entered the room, and he closed his door behind her. She was holding the ring in one hand and Jane Doe's right shoe in the other. "I'm too excited to sleep. Look at this." She handed him the opened ring.

"Pia Lamberti," Bruno said, instantly recognizing the former first lady.

"Where did you get the ring?"

Donais explained, having forgotten to tell her partners about it, given what happened at the morgue.

"And the shoe?"

She opened the platform heel of Jane Doe's right espadrille and removed the micro digital voice recorder, which was the size of a thin matchbox. She handed it to Bruno. "If you look closely, there's a place for a FireWire connector on the side."

"I don't have that type of connector with me," Bruno said.

"Neither do I," Donais added.

"We'll buy one later this morning when the stores open. It'll be interesting to hear what's on this," Bruno said, holding the recorder in his right hand. "You're an amazing investigator, Lisette. Elia and I are fortunate to have you as a partner."

Donais blushed.

"Let's wake Elia. He'll want to see what you discovered." Bruno picked up his room phone and called Donati.

A minute later, there was a knock on Bruno's door. Donati arrived barefoot, wearing slacks and a t-shirt. His hair was a spiky mess, seemingly unable to determine what direction it wanted to go. Donais showed him what she found.

"Jane Doe may have been a spy. Call me suspicious," Donati said, "but I don't think she hid the recorder in the heel of her shoe to take business notes. Maybe Labriola was right when he suspected the two men who took the previous Doe's from the morgue worked for an intelligence agency."

"She could also have been a modern-day Mata Hari," Bruno suggested, referring to the Dutch exotic dancer and courtesan who was a spy for Germany during World War I.

"Why is she carrying a hidden photo of the wife of the former president?" Donati asked. "Either Pia Lamberti knew Jane Doe, or Mata Hari had a fixation with her."

"This will take finesse. We need to question the former first lady and have her answer questions without upsetting her," Bruno said. "Acardi will have to set the meeting since she might not take a call from us."

"She may tell him to twirl on it," Donati said. "Think about it. We want to question the ex-first lady about a photo of her that someone secretly carried."

"It's obvious she doesn't have to take the meeting. But if she does, you're the one to go," Bruno said, looking at Lisette.

"Because you and I are bulls in a china shop," Donati stated.

"Something like that."

Since everyone was wide awake, they agreed to clean up and go to the downstairs lobby, where the hotel kept a large urn of coffee for guests. At 4:45 a.m., the trio was sitting in the bar area beside the lobby when Bruno called Acardi and told him what Lisette found.

Acardi entered the hotel at 6:10 a.m. and found them at a table in the breakfast room, which opened ten minutes earlier. A cup of espresso was waiting in front of the empty chair at the four-top table, and even though it was tepid, he eagerly drained the cup.

"I needed this," he said, signaling the server to bring another. Acardi, like the trio around him, added nothing to his espresso. "Show me what you found," he said, the excitement evident in his voice.

Donais put the recorder on the table. She then opened the ring and placed it beside the device.

Acardi examined both. "Pia Lamberti," he said after seeing the picture.

"There's a possibility she knew Jane Doe," Donais speculated.

"And you want to speak with her."

"We were hoping you could arrange it," Bruno said.

"I can make a request."

"We thought we'd send Lisette," Bruno offered.

"Good choice - if she consents to see her," Acardi cautioned. "What's on the recorder?"

"We don't know. We need to buy a FireWire connector to find out," Donais answered.

"I have one."

"Really?"

"It's in my car. It connects my digital camera to my computer so I can download photos from a crime scene. I'll get it while one of you gets your laptop."

As Acardi left for his vehicle, Donais went to her room. They returned at approximately the same time. Acardi handed the FireWire cable to Donais, who connected one end to the recorder and the other to her laptop. Nothing happened.

"I don't think this device likes your computer," Acardi said to Donais.

"There may be a rechargeable battery inside this recorder," Donais replied. "If so, it'll need a minimal charge before it comes to life. Of course, it could also be dead on arrival after a decade of inactivity. We'll know which in a few minutes."

It turned out that the recorder was not DOA. After being connected to the computer for ten minutes, a message appeared on Donais's laptop giving a particular piece of software needed to interface with the recorder. Donais did a Google search, found it, and downloaded the software.

With the recorder able to sync with the computer, a folder appeared. Donais double-clicked on it. Inside were five long recordings plus one that lasted 20 seconds. Looking at the length, size, and date of the six recordings, she saw they totaled just short of 90 minutes and consumed a gigabyte of memory. The last recording was made on June 14, 2010.

With no one near them, Donais double-clicked on the shortest recording and adjusted the volume to keep it low. When it ended, Acardi was the first to speak.

"The male voice who's asking someone called Carolina to leave the room belongs to Gratiano Riva."

"I think we have Jane Doe's first name," Donais said.

"I agree," Bruno added. "Let's hear the other recordings."

They listened to the remaining five; the restaurant was still not crowded because of the early hour. Acardi gave them the identity of the two voices the trio didn't recognize - Riva and Pagano, while Bruno pointed out Piras. Once the last recording ended, Bruno gave a summation.

"There are three conversations between Riva and Piras. What we heard substantiates what Gentile told us about Heritage Restorations having an inside track on government contracts and change orders. The last two recordings, between Riva and Pagano, prove their collusion."

"The woman called Carolina may have been a spy or an extortionist who was discovered and killed; that's the only two reasons I can think of for her to have a micro recorder hidden in her shoe. We should consider both possibilities," Donati said.

"I'm looking forward to you asking Pia Lamberti about Carolina," Bruno said to Donais. "We need to find out if she knew her."

"You may recall that I requested that the three of you keep your investigation low key?" Acardi said. "So far, it's been about as low-key as a Kiss concert."

"Can you get a meeting with the ex-first lady?" Donati asked.

"As I said, I'll make a request. I know Pia Lamberti. She might meet as a favor for me."

"When do you think that will happen?" Bruno asked.

"She doesn't procrastinate. If she agrees to the meeting and depending on her schedule, it might be as soon as today."

"In the meantime, how do we avoid Pagano?" Donati asked. "He's trying to kill us."

"We don't know if he was after the three of you, Labriola, or both," Acardi said. "Since the attack took place at the morgue, it appears he may have been after Labriola or Carolina's body, and you three may have been caught in the middle of that snatch and run. Of course, given your affinity for attracting trouble, he could have been after the three of you."

"If he's after the body or Labriola, we should be safe," Donati said.

"Safe? No. You're poking your nose into Heritage Restorations, you asked about Jane Doe, and you killed eight men who, we suspect, worked for him. I'd say you moved off Baldassare Pagano's Christmas card list and onto his shit list."

CHAPTER 7

PIA LAMBERTI'S RESIDENCE was the largest in the Parioli area of Rome, an enclave of mansions on magnificent tree-lined streets just north of the Villa Borghese gardens. The 1930s era residences were a magnet for the affluent who wanted to live in the city yet be far enough away from business and commercial areas to have some measure of privacy. The Lamberti estate occupied one side of a short residential feeder street. A 15-foot-high wall encompassed the five-acre spread, and a similarly high twin wrought-iron gate opened to a gravel driveway that led to the mansion.

Donais pulled beside the call box in front of the gates and pressed the button, looking at the camera next to it as she did. Seconds later, a male voice asked her name. Once she gave it, the gates parted. At the end of the driveway, a man in a black suit with a matching tie and a white shirt met her. He had a mic in his right ear. From the bulge on the right side of his jacket, there was little doubt he carried a handgun.

"Ms. Lamberti is waiting for you upstairs in her office," the man said after opening her door and helping her from the vehicle. "Step this way, please."

Donais, who noticed that he was carrying a security wand, did as she was told. The man stopped several feet from the vehicle and ran the wand over her. He then patted her down. It surprised Donais that a man frisked her, but he was professional and didn't grope the statuesque beauty. He next took her tote and went through it, removing the laptop and powered it up to ensure it worked. Satisfied she wasn't a security threat, he escorted her past the guard with an AR-15 assault rifle standing to the left of the front door. Entering the house, they went up the staircase and got off on the second-floor landing, turning right toward a set of double doors. The guard in front of the doors watched their approach.

The three-story mansion had 13,000-square-feet of living space, the exterior reflecting the Italianate style, meaning it combined the 19th-century phase of classical architecture with stylistic features of the 16th-century renaissance. It had prominently bracketed cornices, a campanile or bell tower at one end, a belvedere or structure meant to take advantage of the view at the other, and adjoining arched windows.

The bottom floor of the residence had the laundry and other service rooms, a well-equipped kitchen, a dining room with a rectangular table that seated twelve, a well-vented cigar room with an adjoining wine vault, and a living area with large windows that offered a view of well-manicured lawns. A covered patio was to the right of the view windows.

The second floor housed a small movie theatre, an elegant wood-paneled library, and massive his and her offices. Although her husband was dead, Pia Lamberti kept his office the same as it was the last day he was in it.

The master bedroom suite and guest rooms were on the third floor.

The basement - large, stark, and unpainted was accessed from an interior staircase or an outside set of stairs.

The double doors leading into Pia Lamberti's office were closed as Donais and her escort approached.

"Wait here," the guard escorting her said as the man in front of the doors opened them to let him enter.

The doors remained open.

Donais didn't mind waiting, fascinated with the magnificent space before her. The white coffered ceiling, a series of sunken panels in the shape of an octagon, was bordered by 20-inch-wide triple-crown molding whose design matched the 12-inch-tall high trim profile baseboard that circumvented the room. The floor was Brazilian cherry hardwood, over which were placed several black and gold patterned Persian rugs. In the center of the room were two plush white sofas which faced each other, with an equally plush chair of the same white fabric at either end. An elegant low-rise antique table was between the sofas. The setting rested on one of the Persian rugs. There was an extensive number of green plants throughout the office, which provided a sense of serenity. Donais had seen less spectacular rooms on the cover of *Architectural Digest*.

She watched the person who escorted her go to the left corner of Pia Lamberti's office and walk behind a six-foot-wide wall of Madagascar areca palms. Through the fronds, Donais saw part of an antique desk, and behind it a woman sitting in front of a laptop.

Pia Lamberti stood and stepped from behind the palms, walking to Donais and extending her hand. The five-foot, six-inch tall woman, with black hair and soft brown eyes, was stylishly dressed in a dark business suit, a white silk blouse, and Valentino Rockstud T-strapped pointed toe pumps. Adorning her neck was a Mikimoto Reserve Akoya pearl necklace. She asked Donais to take a seat on the sofa to her left while she sat in the chair beside it. Since Donais wasn't offered a refreshment, the implication was that Lamberti didn't expect her guest to remain long.

"I believe this belongs to you," Donais said, taking the ring off her finger and handing it to her.

Lamberti took it and, after a brief inspection, put it on the ring finger of her right hand. "Did you open it?" she asked.

Donais said she had.

"Then you know this isn't my ring," she said, pulling the cameo back and looking at the headshot of her that was cut from a larger photo. "One doesn't carry their picture in a memory piece. Where did you find this?"

Donais told her about the discovery of a woman's body behind the wall in President Orsini's office, that the murder weapon was her husband's letter opener, and how she discovered the ring.

"Dante told me most of what you said and that he hired your firm to investigate this murder. That was an intelligent move, given your talents were previously displayed when you and your partners foiled the destruction of the Quirinal."

"You're well informed."

Lamberti smiled. "I was told that the three of you, along with Signor Labriola, had a near-death experience at the morgue. Tell me about that."

Donais unemotionally described the assault, ending by saying she believed Pagano was behind the attack.

"He's a powerful adversary. Perhaps you and your partners should consider life insurance."

"I'd advise him to get some."

"You're my type of woman," Lamberti said with a grin.

"Do you know the name of the murdered woman?" Donais asked.

"Do you?"

"Only that her first name is Carolina."

Lamberti thought for several seconds before taking a deep breath and turning slightly to face Donais better. "Answering questions is difficult for me. I'm suspicious by nature and don't trust someone without a solid basis. I also don't confide in someone unless I have an agenda."

"How do I gain your trust?"

"There are several ways."

"Such as?"

"Knowing you for years, observing how you handle adverse situations, or protecting this country from harm."

"My partners and I have done the latter. But perhaps this will also help," Donais said, opening the tote she set on the floor by her feet and removing her laptop. She then played the conversations that were downloaded from the digital recorder. Lamberti listened intently and without expression for an hour and a half.

"Where did you get those recordings?"

Donais explained.

Lamberti thought for a moment before she spoke. "The woman's name is Carolina Biagi. Her parents died in a car accident when she was 18, and I know of no other family members. She was 22-years-of-age at the time of her death."

"And you gave her the ring."

"Shortly before her death."

"You two must have been close."

"We were lovers," Lamberti said candidly.

Donais didn't want to go down that road and changed the subject.

"Was she an Italian citizen?"

"Yes."

"Her fingerprints aren't in the national database."

"I had them, along with her photo, deleted from every database to which I have access."

"As the wife of the late ex-president, how do you have that power?"

"More on that later. First, I want to compliment you on your Italian. It's excellent for a foreigner. Donais is French?"

"I was born and raised in Paris."

"Do you know why you weren't ushered back to your car once you handed me this ring?"

"Because I'm a charming person?"

"Because you and your partners are in a unique position to help me. I told you earlier - I don't confide in someone unless I have an agenda. In my line of work, I take nothing for granted, and I'm comfortable unleashing violence to attain that agenda." Are you familiar with the Agenzia Informazioni e Sicurezza Interna, or AISI as we Italians call it?

"Only superficially."

"How about the Agenzia Informazioni e Sicurezza Esterna, which most refer to as the AISE?"

Donais shook her head in the negative.

"The AISE is the foreign intelligence service of Italy, which primarily uses human resources to protect our country from external threats. The AISI is their counterpart, which collects intelligence and conducts counter-espionage operations within our borders. Carolina Biagi was an AISI agent. I was her handler."

"You're a spy?"

"I'm this country's intelligence czar, a position I created when my husband became president and which President Orsini kept when he took office. I don't appear on any organizational charts, and my position is considered a state secret. However, I work with so many ministers, high-level government employees, and senior law enforcement officers that it's now a loosely kept secret."

"And Dante Acardi is one of those law enforcement officers?"

"Dante and I had worked together, not only in my current position but also when I was a deputy minister at the Department of Information Security, which oversees the AISI and AISE."

"Why keep the position of intelligence czar a secret?"

"That was my suggestion when I created the job. Inserting me in an organizational chart subjects me to scrutiny by the 945 members of the legislature - that's both the Chamber of Deputies and the Senate of the Republic. It also subjects me to being second-guessed by the President of the Council of Ministers, the Interministerial Committee, and the Department of Information Security - all of which are involved with this country's intelligence. I'd spend my day answering questions rather than protecting this country. As intelligence czar, in what I'll realistically call a quasi-secret government position, I leave that unenviable task to the other directors."

"Yet, with such a lofty position, you were Carolina Biagi's handler."

"Because I was selfish. I was her lover and didn't want anyone else working with her. In a perfect society, I would have divorced my husband, and we would have married. However, with a country that's 80 percent Catholic, and with my position, that wasn't possible. Life is rarely fair."

"You said my partners and I could help. How?"

"The person whom you heard on Carolina's recording is Gratiano Riva,"

"Acardi told us."

"He's young and popular with those under 60. What the public doesn't know, and what the recordings verify, is my suspicion that he's exponentially more corrupt than other government officials. I've suspected for some time, but could never prove, that his rise within the government was because of Pagano culling other rising stars within ministries - killing his opponents and bribing those who could help his ascension. What you played is the first evidence of the association between Riva and Pagano."

"Riva is making him a small fortune by giving Heritage Restorations government contracts and change orders."

"This isn't only about money; it's about power. Pagano wants to put Riva in the president's office. The race is close. It's not beyond the realm of possibility that Riva could win the upcoming election. If he does, the Mafia will control the country for at least the next seven years."

"President Orsini is ahead in all the polls."

"In politics, leads can change overnight. A lie becomes mainstream on social media, an accidental slip of the tongue, or a domestic disaster is blamed on the government. It doesn't take much."

"I assume the AISI can launch a formal investigation of Riva."

"Way too political. With Riva running for the highest office in the land, your recordings will appear to be a setup by the current administration. Riva will say they're fictitious and were put together from fragments of previous conversations. Pagano will amplify that scenario by hiring social media and PR experts who will pummel President Orsini. If I were them, I'd ask to confront the person who supposedly recorded these conversations since that isn't possible. Take it as gospel that no one in the government wants to investigate Riva while he's running for president - and he knows it. The only change to that statement would be documented proof of his corruption from an irrefutable source. The recordings don't fit that criterion."

"As a point of clarity, BD&D is not investigating Riva or Pagano per se. Dante hired us to find who murdered the person I now know is Carolina Biagi. Do you know what her relationship was with Riva? Was she his friend? Substantially more than a friend?" Donais asked, her voice rising slightly at the end of her question.

"His mistress. Carolina was extremely beautiful and always got what she wanted from men, although she preferred women. Once she set her sights on him, he was cooked."

"You told her to become Riva's mistress?"

"Yes. She entered that relationship to document his illegal activities."

"And his wife never suspected he had a mistress? No one knew?"

"It's unknown whether his wife knew about the affair. I'm certain that Baldassare Pagano knew since Carolina lived in the penthouse of one of his residential buildings in Rome."

"And you're not investigating Riva?"

"As I said, that's too political. But I will help with your investigation if it leads to finding Carolina's killer."

"We'll tell Acardi."

"I'll inform him."

"Reading between the lines, if Riva discovers that we're investigating him, we're on our own. The government isn't involved."

"I've never heard of BD&D Investigations."

"What if we investigate Pagano? He obviously has an association with Riva."

"Don't waste your time. I have eavesdropping equipment outside his residence in Tivoli. If I hear anything that will benefit your investigation, I'll pass it on."

Donais didn't comment, believing that Lamberti had no intention of giving her Pagano's unfiltered conversations. Instead, she would only get what Lamberti wanted her to know - which may or may not be an accurate perspective.

"One more thing and this is extremely important," Lamberti said, her face hardening and her eyes locking on Donais with an intensity that frightened her. "When you or your partners find Carolina's killer, don't harm them. Inform me, and I'll handle it."

Donais didn't have to be a mind reader to guess what would happen once Lamberti discovered who killed her lover.

"Give me your cell phone number and that of your partners."

Donais tore a sheet of paper from the notepad in her tote, wrote the information, and handed it to her.

"This is my number," Lamberti said, taking Donais's pen and notepad. "You and your partners need to memorize it and destroy this paper. I'll add the numbers you handed me to my contact list because my phone only accepts calls or texts from known numbers."

When Lamberti stood, indicating that their meeting was over, the man who escorted Donais into the residence, who had been unobtrusively standing at the back of the room, stepped forward and escorted her to her car. Along the way, he spoke into a wrist mic and, as she walked out the front door, her car was waiting with the engine running. Moments later, Donais was on her way back to the Marriott.

"What do you think?" Acardi asked, stepping from an adjacent soundproofed room where a monitor provided him with an audio and video feed of the conversation with Donais.

"You already told me most of what she said."

"And?"

"We have exactly who we need to find Carolina's killer - all without our fingerprints on what happens."

"And Baldassare Pagano and Riva will become casualties."

"Eventually, but not until I'm certain who killed Carolina," Lamberti said.

"I'm surprised you told her about your relationship with Carolina."

"Trust is important."

"Any idea why Pagano sent Bruno the letter and email?"

"It's hard to understand what goes on in the mind of a psychopath. The best I can do is put a bullet into it."

CHAPTER 8

RICCI'S INSTRUCTIONS FROM Pagano on how to dispatch
the three investigators were overkill. In the Mafia
lieutenant's experience, overkill - or using a destructive
capacity above what's required, always succeeded. And, since
the plan only needed a few items, all of which were in Pagano's
residence, there was no delay in when it could happen.

Taking the stairs to the basement, he grabbed his boss's
four-wheel garment bag off a shelf and wheeled it to the back
wall, which had metal shelving bolted to it. He pressed a lever
beneath one shelf, heard a loud click announcing that the
locking mechanism released, and pulled the shelving, along
with the attached twelve-foot-wide section of wall to which
it was anchored, towards him.

The concealed room, which was twelve feet wide, thirty
feet deep, and eight feet high, was brightly lit - the lights
within activated by the same switch that controlled the other
lights within the basement. The room had two sections. The
shelves to the left contained weapons and ammunition. To the
right were explosives, remote and motion sensor detonators,
fuses, and other tools of the trade. Knowing precisely what he
needed, Ricci started on the right and selected parts to build
three devices, which he deftly assembled. Carefully placing

them within the garment bag, he left the room and pushed the wall back until he heard the locking mechanism engage.

Although he didn't know the current location of his targets, he wasn't worried. Since they were from Milan, it was reasonable to assume they were staying at a hotel. If that assumption proved incorrect, he'd try Airbnb and so on until he found them. Eventually, he would. Phoning one of the family's contacts in the hospitality industry, it took less than ten minutes to discover they were at the Marriott Grand Hotel Flora and their room numbers.

Ricci went straight to the hotel and entered the lobby at 4:30 p.m. Wearing a conservative suit and tie and pulling behind him the wheeled garment bag, he looked no different from the other business executives at the hotel. No one paid him any notice as he walked across the lobby and into the restroom. Following the instructions that he received from his contact, he found a master room key taped behind the porcelain fixture in the first stall. He then rolled his suitcase onto the elevator and pushed the button for the fourth floor.

For the past hour, Donais recounted to her partners her visit to Pia Lamberti's residence. As they were discussing this, Bruno received a call from Acardi. The deputy commissioner was in the lobby.

"We're sitting at a table in the bar. Come join us," Bruno said. Several minutes later, Acardi arrived.

"Lisette just finished telling us about her meeting with Pia Lamberti," Donati said as Acardi took a seat.

"I'd like to hear about it."

Donais summarized what he already knew, including that Lamberti told her she couldn't release the recordings.

"Did you know she was the intelligence czar for the republic?" Donais asked.

He confessed he did.

"That's another reason I trust you, Dante. You can keep a secret," Bruno said.

"According to her," Donais continued, "anything to do with Carolina Biagi has long ago purged from every database to which she has access. I got the impression those include databases outside of Italy. I'm not sure I'd take her word on that because she might not want us doing a deep dive into Biagi's life."

"Why?" Acardi asked.

"I don't trust anyone in the world of intelligence. On the rare occasion they don't lie, they skate on the thin edge of truth and hand over a crumb of information every so often to maintain credibility."

"Advice from the NSA?" Donati asked, knowing that Donais was obsessed with the super-secret agency and read everything she could about it.

"Absolutely."

"Pia Lamberti is big on trust. Whatever she told you about Carolina Biagi will be straight down the center," Acardi said. "However, she won't let you see the entire landscape. You discover that on your own."

"Any idea how we delve deeper into the world of Gratiano Riva since Carolina Biagi was his mistress?" Donais asked.

"Piras," Bruno answered. "If anyone knows the minister's dirty laundry, it's him. That said, he may have had a motive to kill Ms. Biagi if he felt she was endangering his boss and could bring down their operation. I'd say we have three solid suspects: Riva, Pagano, and Piras."

"Piras must understand that Pagano will kill him if he confides in us," Donati said. "Therefore, what's his incentive for cooperating, especially if he killed Ms. Biagi and knows that we're searching for the killer?"

"If he killed Carolina, it's unlikely he'll admit it," Acardi answered. "Why would he? As for cooperating and giving us information on Riva and Pagano, the only way that may work is to grant him immunity and put him in witness protection."

"What do we need to do to make that promise and have it happen?" Donais asked, looking at Acardi.

"Get Lamberti's permission."

"Assuming we get it," Donati said, "we should play the recordings for Piras and threaten to send them to the media if he doesn't cooperate. He'll understand that creates two untenable problems - he'll be arrested, and Pagano will kill him so he can't make a deal."

"You can threaten him with that, but it'll be a bluff because you can't release the recordings as it will look like President Orsini is trying to frame Riva," Acardi responded.

"Right," Donati replied, remembering what Donais said earlier.

"We may have another option," Bruno said. "Let's listen to the recordings again to see if we can thread the needle and redact Riva's name and any mention or inference to his ministry. That way, the focus is solely on Piras and Pagano."

Everyone agreed it was worth a try.

"My laptop is in the tote in my room. I'll get it," Donais volunteered.

"Relax," Acardi said. "I'll do it. I have to hit the restroom on the way."

"Use mine."

"That's appreciated. While I'm gone, I wouldn't be opposed to someone ordering me an espresso with sambuca on the side."

Donais handed him her room key, which was inside a cardholder with the room number written on it.

The elevator bank was to the right of the lobby bar and, as Acardi approached, an elevator door was closing. Dashing to it, he extended his arm into the narrowing space between the doors triggering the infrared sensor to reopen them. He entered and pressed the button for the fourth floor.

As he approached Donais's room, which was the third one to the right of the elevator, he saw a *do not disturb* sign on the door handle. Removing the keycard from its holder, he inserted it into the slot and turned the handle - which caused the sign to fall onto the floor. Acardi had many obsessive-compulsive tendencies, one of which was neatness. However, with his left hand grasping the handle and his right holding the keycard, something had to give. Shoving the keycard into his jacket pocket, he bent down, picked up the sign, and pushed open the door in a near-simultaneous move. That action triggered a motion sensor, which detonated the explosive device in the room.

A blast force is a series of three events. The first is the rapid expansion of gases emanating from the explosive material. This spherical wall of gas, traveling faster than the speed of sound, impacts everything within a 360-degree radius. As this wall of gas contacts an object, the surrounding pressure drops and creates a vacuum. Almost instantaneously, the second event occurs - a rush of supersonic wind that's sucked into this vacuum along with the fragments and debris created by the explosion. The wind lifts whatever it encounters, stopping only when it slams into a stationary object. Depending on the type of explosive material and the combustibles surrounding the point of detonation, the last event may cause a fire, searing chemical burns, or asphyxiating dust.

Acardi never saw, heard, nor felt the effects of the blast force and subsequent fire because they occurred within 65 milliseconds, and the minimum time it takes a human to react to any stimulus is 100 milliseconds.

The explosion was the first of three that occurred in rapid succession as the vibration of the fourth floor triggered the motion sensors in Bruno's and Donati's rooms. With the two subsequent explosions, the Marriott shook as if it was the epicenter of an earthquake. Moments later, fire alarms sounded, and pandemonium ensued as everyone ran for the exits, except for three people.

"Dante!" Bruno said, echoing his partner's belief that Acardi was associated with the blast.

Rushing from their table, they worked their way through a wave of panicked people. Eventually, getting to the elevator bank, they found that each of the cars was inoperative and had their doors open. Later, they would learn that, following a seismic event or the activation of the fire alarm, the elevator cars were programmed to descend to the lobby and remain there with the doors open until re-certified for operation.

"The stairs," Donais said, pointing to their right.

Since the elevators were inoperative, the stairways became the only way to descend from the upper floors and leave the hotel. With the fire alarm blaring and the explosions and the shaking of the hotel prominent in their minds, people were in a frenzy to leave the building. It wasn't long before the stairways became jammed with hotel guests, who were descending at a snail's pace as more and more people poured into them.

It was against this wall of frantic, scared, and wailing people that the three investigators ascended to the fourth floor, taking ten minutes before they stepped into the corridor, where they were immediately deluged by water coming from the fire suppression system above them. Slogging through ankle-deep water towards Donais's room, they saw the remains of her door laying askew against the wall across the hallway. Partially visible beneath it and showing no signs of movement was Acardi. After Bruno and Donati lifted the heavy door off him, Bruno knelt and put his fingers to the right side of Acardi's neck.

"His pulse is weak," Bruno said. Removing his cell phone from his pocket, he dialed 118, the number for medical emergencies, and received a busy signal. He then tried 115 for the fire department, 113 for emergency police help, and finally 112 for the Carabinieri, getting a busy tone with each attempt. While he was doing this, Donati and Donais also tried contacting emergency services but didn't get anywhere.

"Our Italian phone system is as ancient as the gladiators," Donati said in frustration. It's probably overwhelmed by the number of calls for emergency services. I'll go downstairs and wait for the first responders. When they arrive, I'll bring someone up here." Donati got up and ran towards the stairway.

"He stopped breathing," Donais said with a sense of urgency as she held a finger under Acardi's nose. Tilting his head back to open his airway, she gave him mouth to mouth resuscitation, and Bruno began chest compressions at a rate of 120 per minute. Acardi took a breath. As he did, the sprinkler system shut off.

Twenty minutes later, Donati returned with two paramedics carrying a stretcher. After a brief examination, one paramedic placed him in a neck collar and put an oxygen mask over his nose and mouth while the other inserted an IV line in his arm. They then placed him on the stretcher.

"Do you need help taking him downstairs?" Donati asked one paramedic.

"We got it," he said, as he and his partner lifted the stretcher with the 164-pound sexagenarian on it and took him away.

Bruno looked at the large, blackened hole that was once Donais's room. The back wall was gone. There were two holes and debris further down the corridor. "Judging from the three near-simultaneous explosions, I'd say the trigger was a motion detector, the vibration from one triggering the other two. A tripwire or remote-control detonator in Lisette's room wouldn't have detonated the devices in ours."

"That should have been me," Donais said, looking at the heavily scarred door to her room under which they found Acardi.

"Don't beat yourself up," Bruno countered. "It's not your fault - it's the fault of the asshole who placed these devices."

"We'd better get moving," Donati interjected. "The state police will question everyone who was in or around the hotel at the time of the explosions. Since the bombs went off in our rooms, they might believe they're ours and detonated prematurely. We may be explaining what happened after we're arrested and thrown in jail. Anything's possible without Acardi watching our backside."

"Two attempts on our lives in as many days," Bruno said.

"Since he tried to kill us at the morgue, we should assume this is also Pagano's handiwork," Donais said.

"I think we agree on that," Bruno replied. "The question is, where do we stay? If he found us here, I'm betting he can find us at another hotel."

"Lamberti may be of help. I can call her," Donais offered.

"Good idea," Bruno conceded. "I'd also like to go to the hospital and check on Dante. If I call, the staff won't tell me anything since we're not related."

"The state police will be guarding him," Donais said. "They won't have to use their imagination to figure out where we've been when they see three dripping wet people walk into the hospital. When they ask for our names, they'll take us in for questioning and throw us in a cell."

"The state police at the hospital will be from the protective detail division, an assignment given to the newest officers because it's as boring as watching paint dry," Bruno said.

Donati conceded the protective detail was his first duty assignment after joining the force.

"We can tell them we're at the hospital being checked out. That's a plausible story," Bruno said. "We should be safe until Lisette speaks with Lamberti."

While Bruno was correct about the composition of Acardi's protective detail, his last statement could not have been further from the truth.

As Bruno, Donati, and Donais exited the hotel, they were being watched by Franco Zunino, a handsome 28-year-old athletic-looking man who wore a dark gray pinstriped suit, white shirt, and pink tie. He was six feet, two inches tall, had short black hair, and a perfectly groomed stubble beard. To those around him, he appeared to be a successful young businessperson who stopped to see what was happening, his piercing hazel eyes giving the impression that he had a serious and focused demeanor.

Fifty feet to Zunino's right, Romelo Ricci also watched the trio leave the hotel. "Figlio di puttana. Tre delle persone più più fortunati del mondo," Ricci uttered to himself after seeing that the three investigators survived and saying that they were the luckiest people in the world.

Ricci and Zunino were in the sizeable crowd behind a perimeter of police vehicles and yellow plastic security tape. Both were there for different reasons. Ricci wanted to see if one or more of the investigators survived since two of the explosive devices he planted went off prematurely. Zunino was there on Pia Lamberti's orders to follow Donais, report her movements, and execute his last resort directive if necessary. Seeing the destruction caused by the blasts, he was just as surprised as Ricci to see Donais walking out a side exit of the hotel with her partners.

The three investigators, drenched by the building's fire sprinkler system, took the blankets handed out by first responders in the lobby and decided they would exit through a side door they saw when they were in the lobby bar. They wanted to avoid the police, who they saw directed those who walked out the front entrance to other officers standing to the right of them. The last thing they wanted was to be questioned. Apprehensive that the police would also be near the exit they were going to use, they breathed a sigh of relief when they opened the door and saw that they were alone.

Wrapping the blankets around them, they speed-walked as they headed for a section of the police perimeter tape that encircled the property but was devoid of law enforcement. When they reached it, Bruno and Donati lifted the plastic tape and stretched it above their heads. This allowed Donais to pass underneath with them following.

One hundred yards ahead of the trio was a four-lane roadway. Although there was no taxi stand in sight, they saw several empty taxis passing near them - all of which failed to stop despite waving their arms and doing everything they could short of sending up a flare. They wanted to go to the Fate Bene Fratelli Hospital, which was less than five miles away, finding out from a paramedic in the lobby that's where he was to take anyone who required hospital care.

When the third empty taxi passed, Bruno looked at himself and then at Donati and Donais. "We look like three soaked vagabonds," he said. "This might take a while."

It did. After Bruno made that remark, 12 taxi drivers sped past them before one stopped and agreed to let them get into his taxi if they put their blankets on the seats so they wouldn't get soaked.

Ricci and Zunino saw the trio walking towards the highway and ran to their cars, Ricci carrying the tote he'd taken from Donais's room, which also contained Bruno and Donati's computers. Both waited in their vehicles as they watched the trio repeatedly attempt to hail a taxi until one stopped. They then followed, both so focused on not losing the taxi that they didn't notice each other.

Pagano called Ricci five minutes after he pulled away from the curb. "I'm looking at the news. There are three rather large holes in the Marriott's fourth-floor facade. I take it the investigators are dead."

"They're alive and unharmed. Someone must have entered one of their rooms and triggered a device. I think that explosion set off the motion sensors on the other devices."

"Cosa devo fare per ucciderli?" Pagano said, asking himself what it would take to kill the trio. "Where are they now?"

"In a taxi. The Fate Bene Fratelli Hospital is ahead. They may be going there."

"I'm familiar with that hospital. On the east side, there is a heavily landscaped area with a parking lot behind it. You can see the main entrance from the bushes without being seen. Keep them under surveillance until Sanna and his team arrives. If their taxi bypasses the hospital and goes elsewhere, let me know, and we'll end it there."

It took 30 minutes in the congestion created by first response vehicles and looky-loos to reach the hospital. As the taxi headed for the main entrance, Zunino took his car to the right and up a road that led to the overflow parking area at the top of a hill. Steps led from there to the front of the hospital. He was familiar with the grounds, having used the emergency room to get his hand stitched following a knife wound. He'd also driven others there to get patched up. Lamberti had a special relationship with the hospital administrator who kept the agents working for her or the AISI or AISE, and their medical records, out of the hospital's database.

After parking his car, Zunino opened the trunk and lifted out a case containing an L115A3 sniper rifle with X-Sight 4K Pro thermal night vision scope. The scope took the guesswork out of night operations, exposing the thermal signature of those who believed they were undetectable because they were hiding behind something, and it was night. The scope also provided the range, wind, temperature, humidity, and angle to the target. After inserting a magazine containing 8.59 mm bullets, which were heavy enough not to be deflected at an extensive range, he sighted on the sliding glass doors at the front of the medical facility and waited to execute his last resort directive.

Although the hospital was busy, it wasn't overly so. Most cars discharged their passengers near the front entrance or at the emergency room, which was around the corner and had its own access beneath a porte cochère. Afterward, drivers would park in the main parking structure 50 yards to the left of the front entrance. Zunino discovered the overflow area when he tried parking in the main lot, and it was full. He was told to go to the overflow or the east lot. He chose the lot at the top of the hill because it was slightly closer.

The Jeep Compass carrying Saana and his men went, as Pagano directed, to the east side of the property and parked in the lot behind the thick landscaping. Two minutes later, Ricci's Mercedes E 450 left that same area.

Zunino, suspicious of why two vehicles would park so far away from the hospital entrance, focused his scope on the thick landscaping, where he saw the thermal signatures of four individuals within dense shrubbery - invisible to the naked eye but not his X-Sight. Each held an automatic weapon, which they pointed at the front of the hospital. Zunino had a good idea who they were there to kill.

The trio appeared in the glass corridor leading to the exit ten minutes later. As they approached the front entrance, the four opened fire. Bruno, Donati, and Donais fell hard and showed no movement as they lay haphazardly sprawled within a mass of broken glass intermixed with chunks of concrete and shards of plastic.

CHAPTER 9

Z UNINO LOOKED THROUGH his scope and saw the four men stand and reload their weapons as they exited their hiding place. Since they were moving away from the parking lot, it was clear that they were going to check the bodies and ensure that none of the investigators were still breathing. He didn't know whether they were dead or badly wounded. The last resort directive from Lamberti called for him to eliminate anyone who attacked or posed an imminent threat to the three investigators. Unfortunately, he was too slow to respond to the threat and the investigators paid the price.

Sighting on Sanna, the shooter to the far right, he put a round in the center of his face and, a second later, the face of the person next to him. Both men fell backward into the shrubbery. The other two men seemed to get the message that their status changed from predator to prey. They scrambled into the center of the shrubbery and kept low, believing that the leafy vegetation made them immune from detection. Zunino proved that assumption wrong when he put a bullet in the left side of each of their backs, the bullets exiting their chests after penetrating their hearts.

Bruno, Donati, and Donais got off the hospital elevator with a look of frustration on their faces because no one would give them Dante Acardi's condition. On top of that, Donais's calls to Pia Lamberti had gone unanswered. Deciding to wait in the hospital lobby until the shift change to see if they could convince someone on the incoming staff to give them information also turned out to be a bust when security told them only those who required medical services and family could wait there after visiting hours. With no other alternative, they called it quits.

"Any ideas where we can stay?" Donati asked.

"Any place where we can get a few hours of sleep without someone trying to kill us," Donais answered.

"Thinking about it, we already have a secure place to stay," Bruno said, bringing a quizzical look from his partners. "Each of us has an unrestricted access pass to the presidential palace. We'll be safe there."

"It's not a hotel; where do we bed down?" Donati asked.

"In the conference room that DeRosa let us use. Besides, we don't have another option until Lisette can get ahold of Lamberti."

With everyone agreeing they'd be safe at the Quirinal, Donati used an app on his cell phone to summon a taxi. "Ten minutes," he said. Let's go outside and get some fresh air.

Some assume that you can hear the report of a rifle, getting a heads-up before the impact of a bullet. However, hearing the round exploding from the barrel and experiencing its impact occur almost simultaneously with the shot hitting a person before it's possible to react to the sound. Fortunately for the trio, Pagano's men had sophisticated laser-sighted weapons, which shone a bright red dot on the intended point of impact. Therefore, as the investigative trio made its way to the hospital exit with Bruno in the center, he noticed red dots on his partner's chests and roughly pushed them to the ground. A fraction of a second later, the timing so close that it looked as if gunfire killed the trio, bullets pounded the area and pulverized everything within a gnat's whisker of them.

"Stay down and don't move," Bruno said. "We have to make them believe we're dead - or we will be."

"Hopefully, hospital security heard the gunfire and get here before the bad guys check if we're dead," Donati whispered.

"Hopefully," Donais repeated.

They maintained their positions on the rubble-strewn floor, not knowing whether there would be a second barrage, whether the gunmen would come and confirm their deaths, or if the police would arrive.

Two minutes after the gunfire ended, a police vehicle, with its LED lights flashing and siren shrieking, pulled outside the now destroyed hospital entrance. Other sirens could also be heard in the distance. As the trio faced the shattered entry doors, two uniformed police officers, handguns drawn, cautiously approached them. Seeing the officers, the three investigators stood, brushed fragments of glass and other debris off themselves, and gave them their names. As they relayed what occurred, security guards from within the hospital arrived in force.

The trio had just finished giving their version of the assault when a man in a dark suit and tie, with a chief inspector's badge affixed to his belt, entered the building. The two uniformed officers who took their statements noticeably straightened their posture as he approached, and one gave the chief inspector a shortened version of the trio's story.

"Chief Inspector Bruno, Chief Inspector Donati, and Ms. Donais?" the chief inspector asked.

"Former chief inspectors," Bruno said, extending his hand in the spirit of camaraderie only to have a handcuff placed on it. The chief inspector directed the two uniform officers to handcuff Donati and Donais.

"What's this about?" Bruno asked.

"The three of you have warrants for your arrest on charges of terrorism and attempted murder. Specifically, the detonation of explosive devices in a public place with the intention of causing mass casualties. You're also charged with the attempted murder of Deputy Commissioner Acardi."

"The same person who tried to kill Acardi tried to kill us because Dante hired our firm to solve a case for him. If you don't believe me, you can verify that with President Orsini."

"This is getting interesting," the chief inspector said sarcastically. "The number two person in the Polizia di Stato employs an outside investigative firm from Milan. He does this, even though he has thousands of police officers and inspectors working for him because either your talents are so extraordinary, or he can't trust anyone in the Polizia di Stato. What you're doing is so sensitive that the president himself is involved. I'm sure the judge will enjoy your story as much as your cellmates. Frisk them," the chief inspector said brusquely to the uniformed officers, who confiscated three handguns from the trio.

"When we get to the station, I'll call President Orsini and straighten this out," Bruno said to the chief inspector as he was being led to a squad car while Donati and Donais went to separate vehicles.

"As a former chief inspector, you should already know terrorists don't get to make calls. That way, they can't warn other terrorists." The chief inspector walked closer and put his face a scant inch from Bruno's. "I've known the deputy commissioner for years. You'd better pray he doesn't die. If he does, the three won't make it to trial."

It surprised Zunino that the three investigators were unharmed. It surprised him more when he saw them being handcuffed and taken away. Deciding it was time to leave before the arriving police locked down the area surrounding the hospital, he returned to his vehicle and placed his rifle and scope back in their case.

Traffic had cleared of the congestion caused by the Marriott bombing, and he got to Lamberti's residence in around 25 minutes. He went to her office and found her sitting at her desk.

"I don't have to ask how it went," Lamberti said upon seeing Zunino. She stood and went to her customary chair between the sofas. "I received a call from the commissioner saying that the police found four bodies with automatic weapons in the shrubbery to the east of the hospital entrance. He believes they're responsible for trying to kill the investigators because of the number of shell casings around them. What he's confused about is who killed them and why. However, when he discovers they're associated with Pagano, which I'll help him with if necessary, he'll stop looking for answers beyond the Mafia chieftain. Now, tell me what happened."

Zunino did.

"You carried out my directive to perfection."

"We're lucky Pagano didn't hire Vespa," Zunino volunteered. "If he had, the investigators would be on their way to the morgue."

"A mistake that I'm sure he regrets."

Vespa was rumored to be Pagano's favorite assassin, who had a mythological reputation for never failing. No one had information on the killer, including their appearance. What Lamberti and the police knew about Vespa was second or third-hand information.

"What do you want to do about the investigators?" Zunino asked. "They're in jail."

"I'll call the commissioner and tell him they arrested the wrong people and, in their zeal, let the perpetrator of the explosions getaway. That should make him feel good."

"What if he wants to investigate what they're doing in Rome?"

"I'll discourage that. The commissioner and I have had our tugs-of-war in the past. He's a politician who should have retired years ago. But he's also a survivor. He doesn't gain political capital by arguing with me; he loses some. He'll go along to get along."

Lamberti stood.

"You did well, Franco. The investigators are at the city jail on the via Bartolo Longo. By the time you get there, they'll be released. Bring them here."

At 10 p.m., Zunino led the trio into Lamberti's office. As she introduced herself to Bruno and Donati, she couldn't take her eyes off their wet, disheveled, and soiled clothing.

"It looks like you've had a rough day," she quipped, asking them to remain standing while Zunino retrieved three folding chairs from the basement.

Bruno and Donati marveled at the room as they waited for him to return.

"White must be your favorite color," Bruno said.

"Which is why the three of you will sit on folding chairs."

When Zunino arrived with the chairs, everyone sat.

"I'm assuming you were instrumental in the police releasing us," Bruno said.

"Obviously."

"I'm also assuming the reason we're alive is that you had us followed, and your shooter killed whoever was firing at us."

"Franco Zunino, the person who brought you here, saved your lives. He followed you from the hotel to the hospital and killed the four assailants shooting at you. I told you that in my line of work, I take nothing for granted," she said, looking at Donais, "and that I was comfortable unleashing violence if it suited my purpose."

"And keeping us alive suited your purpose?" Donati asked.

"For the moment. However, keeping the three of you alive long enough to find Carolina Biagi's killer may not be possible. Pagano employs a particularly competent assassin who could easily kill all of you. For some inexplicable reason, he hasn't given them the contract."

"How do you know?" Bruno asked.

"Because you're still alive. With three attempts on your lives in two days, it's a certainty that Baldassare Pagano wants to kill the three of you. Thankfully, he used in-house resources in those attempts. Why do the three of you scare him?"

"How do you know it was Pagano who tried to kill us tonight?" Donati asked.

"Call it a hunch based on the attack at the morgue. When the police identify the four bodies, I'm certain they'll link them to his employ."

"When will you know?" Donais asked.

"Tomorrow. Let's go back to the beginning. I need to understand why he wants you dead. Tell me everything the three of you did from the moment Dante visited your office in Milan until you were arrested. You start," Lamberti said, looking at Donais.

For the next 40 minutes, Donais detailed their movements and conversations. When she finished, Lamberti asked if Bruno or Donati had anything to add. They didn't.

"How is Acardi?" Donais asked.

"He survived surgery and is unconscious, but his doctors are uncertain if there's neurological damage. Given his proximity to the blast, they believe it's a distinct possibility. Therefore, his prognosis is uncertain."

"Surgery?" Donati asked.

"His spleen ruptured. He may also have other issues, beyond the neurological damage, from the trauma of the explosion."

Bruno looked as if he took a gut punch, while Donati and Donais were visibly distressed. "Will he make it?" Bruno asked.

"It's uncertain. But he has the finest doctors in the country looking after him. Getting back to our discussion, why do you believe Pagano wants you dead?"

"Because of our investigations of Heritage Restorations and Carolina Biagi," Bruno answered.

"I concur. But the bigger picture is that he wants to put Riva in the president's office, and your investigations could torpedo that ship before it sails."

"Now might be a good time to tell you that the micro-recorder, and the computer on which I downloaded the recordings, were destroyed in the explosions at the hotel," Donais said.

"The recordings are gone?"

"The recorder and computer are, but I believe those digital files were automatically uploaded to the cloud when I connected to the hotel's Wi-Fi system. I store all my files on the cloud."

Lamberti looked admiringly at Donais. "Let's see if they are," she said. Leading Donais to her desk, she turned on her internet computer. Ten minutes later, they returned with a flash drive containing the recordings.

"Although I can't publicly release these recordings for the reasons I previously mentioned to Ms. Donais, I plan to leverage them," Lamberti said. "I've arranged for the three of you to meet Riva in the morning. As Lisette was downloading the recordings, I texted him and arranged for breakfast at the Ministry of Infrastructure and Transport at eight sharp."

"Because we need to move our investigation along. And there's no telling how much longer we'll be alive with Pagano, and probably Vespa, coming after us," Bruno said, Looking at Lamberti.

"Exactly. Therefore, since time is of the essence, what will you do when you meet Riva?"

Bruno thought for a moment before responding. "The recordings should rattle him. I want to see his reaction when he hears her voice, and I tell him that her body was found. We'll find out where that takes us."

"He won't have any idea what the three of you know about Carolina's murder. That will be unsettling and intimidating. You're wild cards and unpredictable."

"And you think he'll make a mistake and reveal something in his conversation with us because he may be unsettled and intimidated?" Donais asked.

"I'm counting on it. He knows something. How you get that information is in your hands - for now."

Bruno looked at the flash drive of the recordings that Donais retrieved from her cloud storage. "Perhaps I can offer a second approach to get information from Riva," Bruno said.

"Tell me."

Bruno explained.

"Brilliant. Do it. Can it be done before your meeting?"

"That all depends on if you can get me cannoli and Red Bull at this hour."

Lamberti didn't bother asking what he meant but told him she had both in her refrigerator. "You need to get moving. Your meeting is in a little over nine hours."

Zunino cleared his throat and plucked at his shirt.

"Good point, Franco. I can't have you three walking into the ministry looking as you are. Riva won't take you seriously. Franco will bring you to a store to get business and casual attire, along with personal items."

"No store is open at this hour," Donais said.

"We have a special relationship with a particular store that allows us to do after-hours shopping. Did the police return your weapons?"

Donati said they did and that her guards had them.

"You'll be staying here as my guests. Go with Franco," Lamberti said as she stood and went back to her desk.

"Do you feel we're pawns on Lamberti's chessboard?" Donati whispered to Bruno.

"Yes, and let's hope she doesn't want to sacrifice us to get what she wants."

Ricci, who had a police scanner in his vehicle, knew only a part of what happened at the hospital before he arrived at Pagano's residence in Tivoli, explaining to his boss what he'd heard. After a call to an informant in the state police, he knew the rest and discovered that, although the three investigators were arrested, the commissioner of the Polizia di Stato ordered their release. The informant didn't know why, although he said that the chief inspector who arrested them was royally pissed when he found out.

"Why won't they die?" Ricci asked.

"Eventually, they will. Luck is transitory. Given time, determination, and money, anyone can be killed."

Pagano took two cigars from his humidor and handed one to Ricci. After they were lit, the two sat in opposing leather chairs.

"You said my men hid in the bushes, and the takedown was to occur as the investigators were leaving the hospital."

"Yes."

"My men had automatic weapons. If the investigators were armed, they'd have handguns - which wouldn't have the range or accuracy to kill my men even if they could see them. A mismatch."

"Yes."

"The only logical conclusion is that, like you, someone followed them to the hospital. Unlike you, they were there to protect them."

Ricci admitted it was the only scenario that made sense.

"As to who sent that person, I would have said it was Dante Acardi, but he's incapacitated, as far as I know."

For the next 45 minutes, Pagano and Ricci threw around a couple of names but eliminated them for one reason or the other, the name of the trio's guardian angel only becoming apparent with the text Pagano received from Riva.

"Riva is having breakfast with the investigators tomorrow morning. Pia Lamberti arranged it. That explains who's protecting them and where they're staying."

"What should we do?"

"I'm not eager to lock horns with that witch. Orsini has given her too much power," Pagano said as he showed Ricci the text. "She set that meeting for a reason, and whatever its purpose, it will not be for either my or Riva's benefit."

"I might have a clue what the meeting's about," Ricci said as he went to the back of the room and retrieved Donais's tote. "I took the computers from the investigator's rooms. A micro-recorder was in the woman's bag," he said, placing the computers and the recorder on the desk.

Pagano powered up the laptops but couldn't access them because they were password protected. "Let me make a call," he said.

Once the call ended, he placed the computers on a side table and looked closely at the recorder. Seeing a headphone port, he plugged a headset into it and listened to the recordings. His ordinarily stoic expression was replaced by one of deep concern. He gave Ricci a summary of what he'd heard. His lieutenant was visibly upset.

"Hold off killing the investigators," Pagano said. "Instead, bring them to me. I want to ask who else heard these recordings, if they have any other secrets they're withholding, and what the witch knows."

"Do you want them brought here? To your townhouse in Rome? The safe house?" Ricci asked.

"The safe house in Guidonia."

"How do you want the grab to happen?"

Pagano told him.

"Easy to arrange."

As they relit their cigars, which had gone cold during their discussion because neither took a puff to keep the tobacco burning, the computer tech that Pagano summoned arrived and was escorted to his study.

"Unlock those laptops so that I can look at the data," Pagano said, pointing to the table near him on which he stacked the computers.

The tech, who performed computer hacking for Pagano in the past, wasn't much of a talker. Without responding, he sat down at the table and began on the first laptop after taking a tool and two electronic devices from his computer bag. Neither Ricci nor Pagano spoke while the tech was working; both focused on enjoying their cigars. By the time the cigars got down to the nub, the tech had handed Pagano Donais's computer, which was at the top of the stack. Pagano looked at her data, finding the recordings in a desktop file.

An hour later, the tech handed over the other two computers. Pagano then went to his desk, withdrew a fat envelope of cash, and gave it to the man. Once he left, the Mafia chieftain methodically went through both laptops.

"Anything?" Ricci asked once his boss finished looking through the data.

"A word search turned up nothing on Riva or me."

Pagano reformatted the three hard drives.

"Smash the computers and recording device and bury them where they won't ever be found. Having them implicates me in the bombings. In a day or two, I'll have you dig three significantly deeper holes in Guidonia after I've reformatted the investigators," Pagano said with a laugh.

CHAPTER 10

▌NDRO MONTANARI WAS five feet, six inches tall, and
anorexic by Italian standards, weighing only 130 pounds.
The 34-year-old, who had short black hair and wore
rectangular-shaped black Balenciaga glasses, lived alone in
a modest two-bedroom condo in the Prati neighborhood of
Rome, which was close to the Vatican-his largest client. The
electronics and computer savant's firm, New Life Consulting,
in which he was the sole employee, designed systems to
protect clients from those who wanted to steal their physical
and electronic valuables.

Protecting another's valuables wasn't always his business
model. Not long ago, the reformed thief broke into the same
vaults and computer systems that he was now hired to protect
and became very wealthy. One day his life took a dramatic
turn when he was caught by Chief Inspector Mauro Bruno -
the result of touching the wrong contact on a cipher lock
circuit board and setting off a silent alarm. That was when
he discovered he needed glasses.

Given a five-year sentence, he had just completed his
second year of incarceration when Bruno called the prison
and ordered that he be taken to a private room and given a
cell phone, at which point he asked the thief how he could

break into a sophisticated vault - the very thing for which the savant was sent to prison. Montanari, marveling at the irony, provided the information, enabling the chief inspector to recover treasures stolen from the Vatican. In return, Bruno arranged for the commutation of the savant's sentence.

Since that time, the two maintained a love-hate relationship - with Bruno frequently asking the former thief to dip his toe back into the waters of illegality. Although Montanari always granted these requests, he dreaded every time Bruno called or visited because he couldn't refuse the person who changed his life.

At 1:30 a.m., Montanari heard someone knocking at his door. He ignored it until his cell phone rang and, looking at the caller, saw it was Bruno. Getting out of bed wearing dark blue boxer shorts and a white t-shirt, he looked through the peephole of his front door and, seeing that it was Bruno, Donati, and Donais opened it. The three investigators entered, each dressed as if they were going to a business meeting. Donati, who was carrying an opaque plastic bag, went to the savant's desk and, removing the half a dozen cans of Red Bull that were in it, placed them beside the savant's computer. As he was doing this, Bruno opened the box he was carrying, showing 15 cannoli. Both Red Bull and cannoli were Montanari's kryptonite.

"How did you find cannoli at this hour of the morning?" Montanari asked, taking one from the box and biting off a third of the tasty Italian pastry.

"The person in whose house we're staying had a supply in one of her refrigerators. She's also addicted to them, as well as Red Bull," Bruno said, handing the box to him.

Finishing the cannoli in his hand, Montanari grabbed another and then opened a can of Red Bull. "What illegal activity do you want me to perform?"

The three investigators sat down on the couch.

"I need you to hack two computers," Bruno said.

"Whose?"

"Gratiano Riva and Baldassare Pagano."

"A presidential candidate and a Mafia don. You understand that if Riva catches me, I'll go to jail, and no one will commute that sentence? If Pagano finds out, he'll kill me. Either way, my life is over if I'm discovered."

Donais, hearing his reaction, left the couch and came to within a foot of where he was standing. The can of Red Bull, which was halfway to Montanari's mouth, didn't complete its journey as the savant set it and the cannoli on his desk. The attractive blonde, who some believed to be a doppelganger for Jennifer Aniston, held his hand as she explained why this was important for the future of Italy. Seconds later, he agreed to help.

"He'll probably have anti-virus or malware software on his PC," Donati said.

"Like what you purchase for €50 in the expectation that it will protect you from Armageddon? I see that crap every day. I know how it works and how to get around it. No civilian or government security software will detect or protect them from what I write."

"You're an angel," Donais said, giving him a kiss on the cheek - which made him blush.

The trio entered the lobby of the Ministry of Infrastructure and Transport at 8 a.m. sharp after only three hours of sleep, having stayed with Montanari until he handed them the flash drive containing the software they needed. After passing through a metal detector, they veered left and went to the registration counter, giving their names and presenting identification to one of the three uniformed officers. The officer typed their names into the system and, seeing their appointment was with the minister, came from behind the counter and escorted them to Riva's office.

Taking an elevator to the top floor, he brought them to a set of highly polished mahogany doors. Riva's name and title were on a heavy brass plaque to the right. The guard opened the righthand door and directed the trio to enter.

The office was enormous, with dark antique wooden flooring from end to end over which were placed intricate oriental carpets. The ceiling was yellow, bordered by thick layers of white wood molding. A large Murano chandelier hung in the middle of the room.

"Welcome," Riva said, extending his hand as he approached the trio.

Seeing this, the guard left to return to his duty station.

Riva directed them to the rectangular conference table to their right, which had five place settings. There was no need to ask who the fifth person would be as a woman came from the back of the office and introduced herself as Gabriele Riva.

"I've never received a text from Pia Lamberti so late at night," Riva began once everyone was seated. "I assume what you came to discuss is extremely important. We can have that discussion before or after breakfast."

When Bruno said before, Riva removed a cell phone from his jacket pocket and told the person at the other end that they'd eat later and were not to be disturbed.

"I believe you'll find what's on this flash drive to be of interest," Bruno said, handing it to Riva.

"What's on it?"

"It's personal and self-explanatory."

Riva rose from his seat and went to his desk. Removing from his black Prada Logo Plaque briefcase the laptop which contained his personal data, he fired it up. Like those at the other ministries, his ministry computer would not accept downloads from an external device. Bruno and Donati worked for the government long enough to know that. Riva could have summoned the IT person to his office to run a series of tests on the drive to ensure there were no hidden programs. Once cleared, they'd download the data into the system and give Riva exclusive access to it. The reason Riva didn't do this was that he suspected techs couldn't resist looking, or in this case hearing, the data he asked them to clear, or that there was a way they could look at the information later without him knowing about it. Since Riva didn't know what was on the drive, he wasn't about to let a tech touch it.

Riva inserted the flash drive into his personal computer and listened to portions of the recordings, fast-forwarding through most of them. He returned to the conference table, leaving it in his laptop.

"We know three conversations were with Sebastiano Piras, and two are with Romelo Ricci. They show the extensiveness of your corruption," Bruno said once Riva sat down. "We also know that the woman's voice on the short recording was Carolina Biagi, whose body was recently discovered at the Quirinal."

"Who made these recordings?"

"Ms. Biagi."

That statement didn't surprise either Riva or his wife, their faces displaying an unnatural calmness.

"How did this come into your possession?"

"We discovered the recorder and brought it to Pia Lamberti."

"What does she want?"

"You can speak to her about that. We were hired to find out who killed Carolina Biagi," Bruno said, throwing the corruption issue back in Lamberti's lap. "We know she was your mistress. I'm sure your wife isn't happy with that lapse in judgment, nor that you're the prime suspect. Did she know too much, or was she going to tell your wife? Which was the reason you killed her?"

"He didn't kill her because being his mistress was inconsequential. I knew about Ms. Biagi and approved of her."

Bruno, Donati, and Donais appeared surprised by the revelation.

"I knew about and condoned all of my husband's mistresses."

"Why?" Donais asked.

"I know my physical limitations. Since I'm not as beautiful as you or my husband's playthings, I didn't want to deprive him of these physical pleasures. We have an agreement: I don't object to his extracurricular activities as long as he doesn't embarrass me with his dalliances in public."

"Her death seems convenient with your husband running for the presidency. That's a motive for murder," Donati added.

"All you have to do is prove it."

"What do you get out of your marriage?" Donais asked.

"Respect, and the knowledge that someday I'm going to become the first lady of Italy."

"The polls show that won't happen."

"Polls change in an instant," Gratiano Riva said. "If these recordings get out, I'll say that President Orsini sent the three of you to extort my withdrawal. I'll ask you to produce the device from which the recordings came. If you can't, and when Piras denies he had these conversations with me, I'll say President Orsini ordered the creation of these recordings and that they were digitally spliced from my previous conversations."

"How do you know we don't have the recorder?"

Riva smiled, and the trio understood he knew they didn't have the device.

"Getting back to your mistress, that you had one won't play well in a Catholic country," Donais said.

"You're right. Then it will have to be President Lamberti's mistress. What if I accused him of killing Carolina Biagi and hiding her body during the restoration, believing she'd never be discovered? Pia Lamberti will have to defend that accusation."

"Who killed Carlina Biagi?" Donais asked.

"You tell me."

"I'm curious," Bruno said. "What's your plan to close the gap with the president, assuming the recordings and Ms. Biagi aren't publicized?

"I'm going to reveal the corruption that permeates President Orsini's administration. It will all be a fabrication, but the reporters writing about these accusations have been well paid to propagate this storyline and continue it through election day. President Orsini was never going to win."

"We'll make what you told us public," Donais said.

"Who will believe three friends of the president? If you'll excuse me, I need to call my PR firm, send them the recordings, and see how quickly I can film my response to this heinous act by a president desperate to be reelected."

Stepping into the street, Bruno no sooner raised his hand to summon a taxi than one arrived. After the three investigators got into the backseat, Donais gave the driver Pia Lamberti's address. The taxi left the curb and pulled into traffic.

"You have some help today," Donati said, looking at the back of the person seated next to the driver.

"My brother-in-law. He'll be driving a taxi soon and wanted to become familiar with some routes and shortcuts I take."

"Good idea."

As the three investigators sat back and expressed their surprise at what happened in Riva's office, they failed to notice the man beside the driver had turned around and was aiming an odd-looking pistol at them. Bruno was the first to be hit with the dart, followed by Donati and then Donais.

The man calmly put down the dart gun and grabbed the handgun with an attached silencer beside him. He pointed it at the trio. "The Ketamine will take effect in three to four minutes. You can't escape; the doors and windows are locked, so don't try anything stupid."

"Who are you?" Bruno asked.

"Romelo Ricci."

"Looks like the fourth attempt on our lives is a charm," Bruno said.

"Looks like."

The taxi got onto the E80, the trans-European motorway, which was the major thoroughfare to Tivoli. Forty minutes later, the vehicle entered Baldassare Pagano's estate. The trio was lifted out of the taxi and carried to the basement, where each was tied to a chair.

"How large a dose did you give them?" Pagano asked, looking at his captives.

"They should wake up in about 30 minutes."

"Once they regain consciousness, do anything to them you want - but find out what they and that witch know and what she's planning."

"Understood."

"Once you're done, throw them into a deep hole but, as a thank you for all the trouble they're caused, make sure they're alive when you do."

CHAPTER 11

MONTANARI'S TROJAN HORSE program, attached to the initial recording on the flash drive handed to Riva, worked as planned. Seconds after Riva inserted it into his laptop's USB port, it innocuously began sending his files and records to an offshore secure data vault which Montanari controlled. With a can of Red Bull in his left hand and a cannoli in his right, the savant looked at his computer screen, which registered what percentage of the data on Riva's hard drive reached the vault. When that number hit 100, the trojan horse program erased itself.

Montanari called Bruno, but there was no answer. This seemed odd given his early morning visit and his urgency in wanting the program. He tried Donati and then Donais, getting the same results. Curious, he located Bruno by accessing a modified GPS tracking program he'd covertly installed on his phone during his morning visit. Bruno, waiting for him to finish the trojan horse program, never noticed the five minutes his phone was missing from the recharging cable. Montanari did this for defensive purposes - wanting to know when the former chief inspector was in Rome and therefore able to drop in on him unannounced.

"What are you doing at a house in Guidonia?" the savant mumbled to himself, seeing the address pop up on his screen.

Accessing the tracking program's search history, which was short because he'd only installed it early this morning, he saw that Bruno went to a residence in the Parioli area and then to the Ministry of Infrastructure and Transport before going to Guidonia. A few taps on his keyboard revealed that the house in Guidonia belonged to an offshore corporation, while the Parioli property was registered to Pia Lamberti. Hacking into Telecom Italia, the country's largest service provider, he got Pia Lamberti's unlisted home number.

Montanari's cell number was blocked, meaning that *No Caller ID* appeared on the recipient's display screen. He did this because he was highly selective in giving out his number, fearing that someone with his skills could hack his phone, either directly or through his provider. Because of the business that he was previously in, which was being a thief, and his current business, which was protecting people and companies from thieves, paranoia was a part of his life.

The phone number he got from Telecom Italia was Pia Lamberti's landline phone, which had all the anti-spyware sophistication of her cell. Therefore, when he called, the residence phone rang. When *No Caller ID* appeared on the screen, the call automatically went to voice mail - the system preventing any phone number that wasn't on Lamberti's contact list from being connected. Montanari left a message and his number. Five minutes later, Pia Lamberti returned his call.

"Mr. Montanari, I'm Pia Lamberti. I feel an introduction is long overdue as President Orsini told me about your invaluable help in preventing the destruction of the presidential palace."

"I played a minor role."

"You were the lynchpin. Ignoring how you got this number because I'm sure you aren't clairvoyant, why are you calling?"

"As I said in my message, I can't get ahold of Bruno, Donati, or Donais. They're not answering their phones."

"Why is that important?"

"I need to update them on something they asked me to do."

"The trojan horse program."

"Yes," Montanari hesitantly replied, showing that he wasn't aware that Lamberti knew what he'd done. "Aren't you afraid someone is listening to this call?"

"My phone is a landline, and I have equipment here and at Telecom Italia that inform me if someone has tapped into it or if there are listening devices near my residence. I'll take a chance that someone isn't targeting your phone at this precise moment."

"Not within a mile," Montanari confirmed.

"Congratulations. We're both paranoid. They were to phone me when they left the ministry. They may still be there."

"They're not."

"How do you know?"

Montanari told her what he'd done to Bruno's phone.

"Where are they?"

"In Guidonia." He gave the address.

"Are you positive they're at this location?"

"Only that Bruno's cell phone is there."

"I'll take care of it. Can you give me a copy of the data extracted from Riva's hard drive?

"Yes."

"I'll send someone to get it."

Montanari gave his address, although he felt that wasn't necessary.

"Send someone to pick up a hard drive from this address," Lamberti told Zunino, handing him the paper on which she'd written it.

Zunino summoned the guard from outside Lamberti's office and sent him to retrieve the hard drive.

Lamberti was sitting in her customary chair between the sofas when Zunino returned and sat on the sofa to her left.

"Pagano may have kidnapped the investigators, which is why they haven't called. I was told they're at his place in Guidonia, which he thinks no one knows about."

"Assuming they were kidnapped, he'll kill them as soon as he's rung them dry of information."

"I can't let that happen because I still need them. Therefore, I'm going to order the NOCS commander to deploy his hostage rescue team."

The NOCS, short for Nucleo Operativo Centrale di Sicurezza, was the special operations unit of the state police that deployed on short notice to recapture targets held by terrorists, to rescue hostages, and to take into custody or kill dangerous people. They were based in Spinaceto, an urban area of Rome.

"And if Bruno's phone is there and the investigators aren't?"

"Then they're dead or soon will be and of no use to me."

Lamberti took the cell phone off her lap and called the NOCS commander, ordering him to rescue three hostages from Pagano's residence in Guidonia, while cautioning him that this information was based on soft intelligence and that she could not confirm the three would be there.

"What are my instructions regarding Pagano, assuming he's there? Do you want him dead or alive?" the commander asked.

"Protect the hostages. Protect your men. Let the cards fall where they may."

"I understand," the commander replied, reading between the lines that it would be better if Pagano were in a body bag.

Lamberti texted the commander photos of Bruno, Donati, and Donais, taken from the BD&D Investigations website. The commander forwarded them to his team.

"How do you want to handle Riva now that the investigators may be out of play?" Zunino asked.

"I'd like to speak with Sebastiano Piras at Heritage Restorations and find out what he knows about the Piras-Pagano-Riva relationship."

"Pagano will kill him if he discovers he's speaking with you."

"I know. If what he has to say is useful, I'll give him immunity, a new identity, and get him out of Rome."

"If it's not useful?"

"He's on his own."

"Even with immunity, his fear of Pagano may keep him from cooperating."

"Not when he hears what I have to say."

"With all respect, why bother with the investigators if Piras gives you what's needed to convict Riva?"

"Because I'm counting on them to uncover Carolina's killer."

Zunino didn't want to discuss the subject of Carolina Biagi with his boss and changed the subject. "Piras doesn't know what you do and might believe you're incapable of delivering on your promise of immunity. He may think you're the ex-wife of the late president who knows a bunch of officials and is looking to them for a favor."

"I'll deal with that once I know what he has. His cell phone number will be in the government database. Call and have him come here."

"And if he doesn't want to come?"

"Be persuasive."

Zunino got Piras's number and made the call, the conversation lasting slightly more than 20 seconds.

"He's on his way. I got the impression he knows what you do."

The CH-47 Chinook helicopter took off from Spinaceto 18 minutes after Lamberti ended her call with the rescue team's commander. It was 33 miles to Guidonia and the Chinook, a twin-engine tandem rotor aircraft with a max speed of 196 mph, took 15 minutes to cover that distance. Twenty operatives were on board, each wearing combat gear and carrying a Beretta PX4 sidearm and a Heckler and Koch MP5 submachine gun.

While the CH-47 checked nearly all the boxes as the perfect aircraft for this type of mission, it had one drawback: it was loud - 115 decibels loud. In comparative terms, that was equivalent to standing alongside the runway as a Boeing 747 or an Airbus A380 roared past. Therefore, Pagano and most of his security staff heard it some distance away and watched from the house's back porch as the giant unmarked helicopter descended and landed.

Under normal circumstances, the operatives would rappel down a nylon rope when they were over their target. However, in this situation, the pilot saw a group of men standing on the back porch and made a judgment call that anyone who rappelled to the ground would be an easy target if this group turned hostile. Therefore, he elected to set the aircraft down to protect the operatives in the event they were fired upon, at which point they could use the armored aircraft as a shield.

Pagano's standard security staff was ten soldiers, not counting his lieutenant. Seven were with him, two were guarding the prisoners in the basement, and one was monitoring the security cameras. The aircraft commander didn't know that when Pagano saw the unmarked Chinook land, he assumed it was a government aircraft - a fact confirmed when 20 operatives emerged from the rear cargo door. Subsequently, he ordered his men to place their guns on the ground to prevent anyone from taking a potshot at the aircraft or the operatives. With the number of heavily armed men running towards them, that exchange only had one outcome - he and his men would die.

The NOCS commander, who led his operatives onto the porch, ordered Pagano and his men to raise their hands. They complied.

"Frisk and flex cuff everyone," the commander ordered.

Once the outside of the house was secured, the commander divided his team into groups A and B. Group A would take the prisoners to the Chinook and guard them and the aircraft while the other group searched the residence.

The commander considered placing most of his men in Group B. However, since the house wasn't large, he feared deploying too many operatives into such a confined space could cause friendly fire casualties.

The guard monitoring the security cameras in the house saw the helicopter land and men dressed in combat gear exit.

He summarily decided that he didn't want another stint in jail and made a run for it out the back door. Had Pagano not recently cut the brush around the house, which he did twice a year to prevent someone from approaching unobserved, the guard could have crawled away and used the dense undergrowth to mask his escape. However, now that it was stubble on the earth, the guard wasn't hard to spot.

The team's second in command, who was near the helicopter, was the first to spot him and yelled for the runner to stop. When that didn't work, he looked through his scope and put two rounds' inches from the runner's left foot, hoping to give him an epiphany that he could have just as easily put two into him. However, the guard wasn't exactly a Ph.D. and turned and fired two rounds from his handgun at the second in command, both bullets impacting the ground ten feet to his left.

"Did this guy take a stupid pill?" the second in command said to the operative next to him.

The ex-Ph.D. candidate, seeing that his rounds were significantly wide of target, and that the operative had his MP5 aimed at him, finally got his epiphany - realizing that his effective range was 25 to 30 yards, while an assault rifle was around 100. He dropped his weapon and raised his hands.

The two men guarding their prisoners in the basement heard the helicopter and the three shots that were fired. They also heard multiple footsteps on the floor above them. Not knowing what was happening, they assumed the worst - that someone was trying to rescue the prisoners. They drew their weapons from their shoulder holsters and waited.

The basement was a filthy unpainted concrete chamber with dust and cobwebs in every corner and crevice, and LED lights overhead to illuminate the area. It smelled of mold, the sweat of the soldiers who used the area to torture and extract information from their victims, and the vomit, blood, and sweat of those interrogated. Bolted to the ceiling and between two of the lights was a thick wooden crossbeam. Affixed to the bottom of it was a steel roller over which three ropes hung. One end of each rope was wrapped around a cleat bolted to the wall. The other was tied around the wrists of each prisoner. The rope was kept taut so that the prisoners' feet barely touched the floor.

The entry to the basement could be described as a descending chute, having white painted drywall on three sides with an unpainted wooden stairway at the bottom. The chute prevented those entering the basement from seeing all but a sliver of it until they stepped onto its concrete floor, and those within the basement from seeing who was descending. Therefore, neither the two men guarding the prisoners, nor the five officers quietly descending the staircase, knew what to expect until they came into each other's line of sight.

The first two special ops officers out of the chute were hit mid-torso and knocked to the floor by two-round bursts from both guards. None of the bullets penetrated the operative's ballistic body armor, although both were dazed and had the wind knocked out of them.

Both guards had 15-round magazines in their guns, plus one in the chamber. Deciding he wasn't going to wait for the next set of boots to hit the floor, one of the guards sent 10 of his 14 remaining rounds into the chute; the bullets penetrating the drywall as easily as a hot knife went through butter. The other guard, also believing this was a great idea, did the same. That might have nailed the three operatives still inside had they not dropped to a prone position upon hearing the first shots. Subsequently, every round flew over them.

"Let's kill the prisoners and get out of here," the guard who shot first said to the other.

As they turned to carry out the murders, two of the three operatives still within the chute got to their feet and ran out. As they did, they pointed their Koch MP5's in the direction from which the shots into the chute had come. Both guards, stunned that anyone survived the nearly two dozen bullets that peppered the drywall, turned their weapons away from the prisoners and towards the operatives. That didn't work out well, as multiple rounds struck each in the torso. The last man through the chute, seeing the guards were dead and the two operatives were getting to their feet, went to the prisoners. Removing his knife from its sheath, he cut them down.

Bruno and Donati each sported a black eye and had swelling and bruises on both sides of their face. Taken to the aircraft, the medic, an operative in Group A, put them on IVs and handed each cold packs to hold to their faces. During their hospital examination, it was discovered each had two broken ribs. Bruno would later tell Lamberti that Donais was unscathed because Pagano believed they'd eventually tell him what he wanted to know rather than see her go through the same physical interrogation.

As the Chinook lifted off, the three investigators leaned back in their webbed seats and looked at the body bags of the guards who interrogated them, and at Pagano, who was cuffed and bunched together with his men on the steel flooring. The Mafia chieftain returned Bruno's look of ambivalence with a stare of defiance and hatred.

"What are you thinking?" Donati asked Bruno.

"That a cobra will always be a cobra," Bruno replied as he continued to look at Pagano.

"Meaning you keep your distance?"

"Not if you're a mongoose."

"Meaning?"

"I'm done taking shit from him."

CHAPTER 12

MINUTES AFTER THE Chinook lifted off, the team commander called Lamberti and told her the rescue was successful and that his team captured Pagano, Ricci, and eight of their soldiers. The call couldn't have come at a more opportune time for Lamberti because Piras, who sat on the sofa to her left, had just listened to the three recordings of Riva telling him how much he should bid on contracts and the expected monetary value of change orders. Visibly shaken, his hands trembled as he waited for her to finish the call. When her conversation with the commander ended, she redirected her attention to Piras.

"It may interest you to know that Baldassare Pagano, Romelo Ricci, and a number of his soldiers have been arrested."

"On what charge?"

"Kidnapping and torture for starters. Although he's going to jail, that doesn't mean you have to occupy the cell next to them. I could make you the exception?"

"The exception?"

"The person who doesn't go to jail for the rest of their life."

"What do I have to do?"

"Give me irrefutable proof of Riva and Pagano's corruption."

"You have the recordings."

"I want more."

"I can't give it to you."

"Let me give you a preview of what will happen if you don't. You'll be arrested and charged with corruption and fraud, although I don't believe you'll be incarcerated for long because we both know that Pagano will have someone put a shiv into your heart while you're in jail."

"If I give you what you want, the same will happen - just not in jail. Pagano will find me."

"I'll put you in the witness protection program and give you a new identity. You don't have to live in Italy. Pick any country in the EU."

"Pagano will never stop looking for me."

"He'll have bigger problems. If he goes to trial, the other families will give him an early retirement to protect themselves."

Piras ran his hands over his face and took a deep breath. "You're not giving me a choice."

"That's the idea."

"What do you want to know?"

"Everything," Lamberti said, pushing the record button on the digital recorder that was on the antique table in front of Piras.

The Chinook landed on the roof of a hospital where Bruno, Donati, and Donais disembarked through the rear cargo door. As they did, the awaiting medical staff looked into the aircraft and saw Pagano and his men in flex cuffs, guarded by men in military combat gear. Several began taking photos and videos, posting these on social media. Word spread like wildfire throughout Rome that the government had arrested the Mafia chieftain.

With Gabriele standing next to him, Riva saw the social media posts.

"No one will talk," she said. "They'll adhere to omertà - the code of silence."

"Someone will. It's inevitable. People will no longer fear Pagano because he's in jail."

"Then we'll reinstill that fear by getting rid of the weak links."

Ten minutes after the Chinook left the hospital, it set down on the helipad of an off-the-books detention facility in Rome whose signage indicated the building was occupied by the Ministry of Economy and Finance's Department of the Treasury. Therefore, helicopters, armored vehicles, armed guards, and heavy security seemed in concert with that signage. Pagano and his men were brought into the rectangular five-story brick building and taken by elevator to the processing area on the first floor. None of the prisoners, blindfolded before they departed the hospital, knew where they were other than it was a prison.

The Polizia di Stato staffed and monitored the facility where every prisoner was considered a terrorist. This meant their rights were nonexistent, and they were kept incommunicado from attorneys and anyone else who might help their plight. Each would receive a trial, which typically occurred within a week, their guilt or innocence determined by a three-judge panel. When convicted, because there was a 100 percent conviction rate, they would return to their cell, which they occupied 23 hours a day. Only a handful of people outside the prison staff knew this facility existed - one of whom was Pia Lamberti.

It was late afternoon when Zunino accompanied Piras to his house to retrieve the information he said documented Riva's corruption. For years, he carefully maintained a file on his misdeeds with Pagano and Riva. He intended to use it as a stay out of jail and stay alive insurance policy, exchanging it for immunity and witness protection - which is precisely the deal Lamberti offered him. However, when it came time to pull the trigger and barter these documents for their intended purpose, he had second thoughts, fearing that the commission's vengeance would result in the issuance of an open-ended big-ticket contract for his death. That's something he considered inevitable if he used this insurance policy, but it wasn't real until now.

Moreover, there was no clear path that led to the winner's circle. With the choice of either going to jail and being an easy target for the commission's vengeance or relying on the government to keep him safe, he reluctantly chose the latter. Lamberti had given him little choice.

Piras's house was two miles from his office. It had a modern white exterior and a minimalistic white interior. As most of the other homes in the neighborhood looked to have been built a generation before, a good guess would be that he leveled whatever structure was previously there and, after bribing the necessary officials, replaced it with the house he wanted.

"Where are the documents?" Zunino asked, once Piras opened his front door and disarmed the security alarm.

"In my safe," he said as he led the way inside.

Zunino, not trusting the Heritage CEO, withdrew his handgun from its shoulder holster and followed a few feet behind.

The safe was behind a hinged picture on his bedroom wall. Piras opened it, removed a dozen nine-by-twelve-inch manila envelopes with dates written on each, and stuffed them in the black soft-sided bag that was beside his nightstand. After Zunino returned the gun to its holster, he relieved Piras of the bag.

They returned to the entrance and, after the alarm was reset and the door locked, started towards the car. At that moment, Piras suddenly flew into Zunino, who caught off-balance landed on the ground next to him. Confused as to what happened, he looked to his right and saw that the center of Piras's face had disappeared.

Oriana Vespa looked through her scope and saw that the .50 caliber round, fired from her Accuracy International AX 50 rifle and traveling nearly 6,000-feet-per-second, did its job. She looked at the man beside her target, who was lying prone on the ground with his handgun raised in search of the shooter. Nestled in the thick brush on the side of a hill 500 yards away, the assassin knew she was invisible to him without the aid of a rifle scope or binoculars. She was also far beyond the range of his handgun.

The 32-year-old was the primary assassin for the commission, the five members referring to her as their arbitrator rather than using her name. That term always made her shake her head because she viewed putting a bullet in someone as anything but arbitration, which required negotiation.

She could have easily killed the man lying on the ground, but experience taught her that killing someone in addition to one's target could have unintended consequences. Therefore, she gave him a pass. That decision was a game-changer.

Pia Lamberti listened intently to what Zunino had to say, after which she glanced through the contents of the manila envelopes. "There's more than enough documentation to put Riva, Pagano, Ricci, and the other co-conspirators in jail. The trick is, releasing it so that it won't make it seem like Riva was set up."

"How will you do that?" Zunino asked.

"I have an idea. If I'd known earlier that Piras had this documentation, I would have given the investigators some of it to show Riva. That may have pushed him over the edge and gotten him to confess to any number of things, including Carolina's murder, or give up her killer because I believe he knows who did it."

"What do you want to do?"

"I know a cooperative reporter. I'll give some documents to them without making it seem that the president or someone in his administration is behind it. Taking Riva down will be a process. We'll start by getting the public on our side, then we can charge him. If we mishandle this, or Riva is skillful at convincing voters that the president is behind this attack on his character, what we're doing will backfire, and he will step into the office of the presidency."

"Do you think whoever ordered the hit on Piras knew he came to see you?"

"Probably not. I believe he was killed because he was a liability to both Riva and Pagano once the investigators played the recordings to the minister."

"That makes sense," Zunino admitted. "It could have been Vespa."

"If it was, the commission has taken charge now that Pagano is in jail."

"When will you give the documents to the reporter?"

"Tomorrow."

"Riva and Pagano may want to make a deal."

"I have other plans for them. Before then, I need to find out what's on Pagano's computer."

"Where should I send it?"

"Nowhere. We're going to make a house call."

Indro Montanari was stirring a large pot of spaghetti sauce on his stove when he heard a knock at his door. Looking through the keyhole, he saw a five-foot, six-inch tall woman dressed elegantly in a dark business suit with a white blouse. He opened the door.

Lamberti introduced herself as she entered his home without invitation, with Zunino closing the door behind them.

"I felt it was vital that we meet face-to-face. Do you know what I do, Mr. Montanari?" Lamberti asked, setting aside any pretext that this was a social call.

"Indro." He was nervous and cleared his throat. "Not long after I gave you the location of Bruno's cell phone, I saw on social media that he, Donati, and Donais were walking off a military helicopter in which Pagano was cuffed. I suspect you work for one of the government intelligence agencies."

"Close," she said, explaining her position.

That revelation shocked Montanari, his eyes widening and his face expressing wonderment.

"I did a background check on you. You're an enormously talented individual. I want to employ your services. Confidentially, of course."

"With all respect, I don't want to be associated with cloak and dagger individuals," he hesitantly responded. "I only do the occasional favor for Mauro Bruno because I owe him a great deal."

"For getting you out of prison."

"And helping me start this business and getting me my first client."

"The Vatican."

Montanari gave her a curt nod. "If working for you got out, my clients would never believe I didn't share their information with the government. Most would fire me."

"I never accept a negative response to an invitation I've extended."

"This time, you'll have to," Montanari said, feeling braver and his voice getting more robust.

"What I do protects Italy, the EU, and sometimes the world. I'll do anything possible to enhance and strengthen my resources. Adding your capabilities to my team does both."

"I still can't accept your invitation."

"I apologize if I didn't phrase my request properly or put it in the right context. I wasn't extending an invitation. What I meant to say was help me, or I'll put you in jail and crush Bruno and his partners for the illegalities you helped them commit. And, if you think there's going to be a trial in open court, you're wrong. It will be private and in front of a very sympathetic three-judge panel. I hope that clarifies my previous request."

"It does, and I've reconsidered," Montanari said after a moment's hesitation, staring at Lamberti as if she was the devil reincarnate.

"Excellent. Here's what I want you to do. This computer belongs to Baldassare Pagano," she said, as Zunino stepped forward and handed it to the savant. "Break into it, download the contents onto a hard drive, and call this number." Lamberti reached into her jacket pocket and removed a card on which only a phone number was printed. I'll send someone to pick up the computer and the storage device. Do you have a spare hard drive?"

Montanari said he did.

"One last thing. If you find anything on this computer relating to Mauro Bruno or his partners, keep it to yourself. Is that clear?"

"Clear."

"After you do this, I'll have your criminal record expunged - a token of gratitude from your newest client."

"Has anyone told you *no* and not changed their mind?"

"Yes, just before I threw them in a jail cell to reconsider my offer."

Once Lamberti and Zunino left, Montanari booted up Pagano's laptop, discovered that he used the standard intrusion protection program bundled with the computer, and penetrated it in less than five minutes. As he began looking through the file folders, he came upon one labeled *Bruno letter and emails*. When he opened it, he saw the folder contained four items - two images, an email sent by Bruno, and an email from a service provider confirming a logon and password. He opened the images. As he read the first, a pained expression took over his face when he realized this was a letter that Bruno wrote to his late wife. The second image was of a Post-it note on which was written: "I know who killed your wife and unborn child." An email address was given below.

"Mio Dio," Montanari said to himself. He opened the email sent by Bruno.

"Your note said you know who killed my wife and unborn child in 1996. Why are you suddenly contacting me after all this time? Were you present when she was murdered? These are some questions that need to be answered. Please let me know a time when we can speak or a place to meet."

Bruno ended by providing his cell number.

Montanari next looked at the email from the service provider. He knew anyone above the age of six knew better than to store a login and password on their computer. However, Pagano was a couple of generations removed from this reality, keeping the access codes accessible so that he wouldn't forget how to get into the account. Seeing that this provider was where the email provided in the Post-it note was being sent confirmed that Bruno was unknowingly communicating with Pagano.

Needing a break, Montanari returned to the kitchen and the large pot of spaghetti sauce - which was burned but still edible. Every 15 minutes over four hours, his habit was to stir the sauce so that it wouldn't stick to the bottom of the pot or burn, which happened when Lamberti arrived and screwed up his timetable. As he stirred the sauce, he debated whether to tell Bruno what he learned from Pagano's computer, going against Lamberti's instructions, or keeping it to himself. The determinant in making this decision turned out to be the consequences. While Bruno would get mad at him for withholding this information, Lamberti would incarcerate him. Choosing survival, he kept what he discovered to himself.

When he returned to his desk, he copied the folder labeled *Bruno letter and email* onto his laptop before transferring the contents of Pagano's computer onto a hard drive. He then sent a mirror of what was on Pagano's computer to his offshore data vault. Once he finished, he called the number on the card. Thirty minutes later, he handed the laptop and external hard drive to one of Lamberti's guards.

Upon receiving the hard drive, Lamberti removed a laptop from the bottom drawer of her desk and placed it in front of her. Since this laptop had no internet capabilities and couldn't be hacked, she kept her work and sensitive information on it. She had a second laptop, on which stringent anti-hacking protocols were installed, using this to access the internet and receive emails - most of which were encrypted. Twice daily, everything received by this computer was erased by a toxic program that made a reconstruction of the data impossible. Before then, whatever she wanted to keep was downloaded to a flash drive and transferred to her non-internet computer. The procedure was cumbersome and time-consuming, but it worked in keeping her data secure.

Plugging the hard drive that Montanari gave her into the USB port of her non-internet laptop, she accessed Pagano's files. Thirty-five minutes later, she finished. "Nothing," Lamberti said to Zunino in disgust. "There's just the email he sent Bruno and his response."

"He's old school. He prefers to give instructions through a messenger or face-to-face. Do you plan to tell Bruno that Pagano was the one who sent him the letter and note?"

"Not yet. If Pagano murdered Carolina, I don't want Bruno killing him. I want that pleasure."

"How are you going to find out?"

"By letting Pagano and Ricci go free."

"That won't be popular with either the public or the Ministry of Justice. They'll want him behind bars."

"I have a way to get what Pagano knows, but it won't work if he's behind bars." Lamberti then told him what she was going to do.

CHAPTER 13

DANTE ACARDI REGAINED consciousness. Although he had a headache, the doctors said his scans showed there should be no permanent brain damage, and his headache would vanish. The three investigators, although banged up themselves, wanted to see him. Lamberti made that happen.

"You look worse than me," Acardi said, seeing Bruno and Donati. "But, as always, Lisette looks beautiful."

That statement earned him a kiss on the cheek and eye rolls from Bruno and Donati.

"You had a close call, coming within a breath of dying. If it hadn't been for Lisette giving you mouth-to-mouth resuscitation, you'd be dead."

"I regret not being conscious for that," Acardi said, looking at Donais and smiling.

Bruno didn't bring up that he'd given him chest compressions, not wanting to spoil Acardi's vision of Donais with her lips over his.

"I've been trying to recall what happened, but it's a mystery because I can't remember anything from the time I went to Lisette's room until I ended up in this hospital bed. Fill me in."

Bruno did. When he finished, he saw Acardi shaking his head.

"I don't know how I survived. I'm lucky I only fractured my humerus, which I've been told could take anywhere from three months to a year to heal. Now that you know how I'm doing tell me what happened to the three of you."

Bruno cleared his throat and gave the deputy commissioner the unabridged version of what occurred, including the meeting with Riva and their kidnapping, interrogation, and rescue.

"Where is Pagano?"

"They didn't tell us."

"I take it Riva is not in custody?"

Bruno shrugged, indicating that he didn't know.

There was a long pause, after which Acardi asked if he and Bruno could have a few minutes alone.

"I'm going to the cafeteria," Donais said. "I'm famished." Donati said that he'd accompany her and asked if they could bring something back. Bruno and Acardi declined.

Once they left, Bruno pulled a black plastic chair close to Acardi's bed and sat down. "Whatever you have to tell me, Dante, it can wait. You've been through a lot and need some rest. I'm going to join the others in the cafeteria."

Acardi extended his right arm, which had an IV line stuck into it, and grabbed Bruno's wrist. "Don't go. I have a confession to make, Mauro. It's been eating at me since before the explosion, and now it's tearing at me."

"It sounds serious."

"It could end our friendship. I know who killed your wife and unborn child. I knew the identity of the guilty party when I saw you in Milan." Acardi let go of his wrist.

Bruno glared at his friend in disbelief, making a fist and clenching his hands so tightly that his knuckles turned white. "Who did it?"

"Baldassare Pagano. Romelo Ricci was there, although he worked for another Mafia don at the time."

Bruno's eyes narrowed, and his tone with Acardi was harsh.

"How did you find out?"

"Pia Lamberti told me."

"How could she know?"

"She has a very sophisticated eavesdropping device pointed at the window of Pagano's study in Tivoli. A laser picks up the minuscule vibrations that sound waves create on the glass, and a converter transforms these to digital information."

"Then she knows everything that Pagano says."

"I wish that were true, but his house is surrounded by trees - undoubtedly for privacy and to prevent someone from putting a sniper round into him. Only a small study window is in the line of sight from the hill on which Lamberti keeps the equipment. She can only pick up conversations in his study."

When Bruno remained silent, Acardi continued.

"There was a conversation between Pagano and Ricci about the letter and note you received and later showed me. They discussed how they sent it to entice you into a situation where you'd be killed. They also reminisced about what happened the night Pagano murdered your pregnant wife."

"You're an excellent actor, Dante. When I showed you the letter and the note, you had me convinced it was the first you'd heard of either."

Acardi's expression showed Bruno's remarks cut him deeply.

"I couldn't tell you. Lamberti made me promise. You would have killed Pagano and Ricci."

"You're damn right I would."

"That would have compromised our investigation of Riva. You also wouldn't have taken the assignment of finding who killed the woman we now know is Carolina Biagi."

"I'm curious why Pagano kept the letter I wrote to my late wife for decades."

"You'll have to ask him. That never came up in the recorded conversations."

"And Pagano's alive because Lamberti wants to wring him dry of information and use him to implicate Riva?"

"Maybe. She never shows all her cards or completely reads someone in on her intentions."

"What will it take for Pia Lamberti to give him up?"

"You'll have to ask her. But I may give you leverage in your negotiations with her and help your investigation into who murdered Carolina Biagi. Are the clothes that I wore at the time of the explosion in this room, or did they throw them away?"

"I don't know. I'll look." Bruno found them stuffed into a large plastic bag in the cabinet to the right of the door.

"Pull out my suit jacket."

Bruno did.

"My poor Canali suit," Acardi said. "Reach inside the left inside jacket pocket and see if the report I was carrying is still there."

Bruno found it. The ten-page coroner's autopsy report was in excellent condition, protected by the vinyl evidence bag in which the deputy commissioner placed it. He tried handing it to Acardi but was told to hang onto it.

"That's the coroner's report on Jane Doe. I was going to discuss this with you and your partners at the hotel. If you read it, you'll discover something interesting."

"What?"

"There's an anomaly," Acardi said, telling Bruno what he discovered.

The revelation caused Bruno to stroke the bottom of his chin as he thought about the implications.

"This changes everything," Bruno said. "Everything."

Franco Zunino was waiting in the hospital's lobby as Bruno, Donati, and Donais got off the elevator and started towards the information counter to have someone call them a taxi.

"How long have you been here?" Bruno asked upon seeing him.

"A few minutes. Ms. Lamberti would like to see you." Zunino led them to the Range Rover, which was parked just outside the temporary exit to the hospital - a patchwork of plywood and 2x4 lumber hastily put in place following the destruction of the glass portal destroyed by Pagano's men.

During the drive to the residence, Zunino explained what the trio suspected, that it was Lamberti who orchestrated their rescue in Guidonia. He also told them that Pagano, Ricci, and the others were being held in a secure prison, not elaborating beyond that description. Continuing to bring them up to date, he explained what happened at Piras's residence. By this time, they arrived at Lamberti's residence.

"You three certainly have a knack for getting into trouble," Lamberti said as they entered her office. "Have a seat."

They took the same positions on the sofa they previously occupied.

"I understand we're alive because you sent a special ops team to rescue us," Bruno said. "Thank you seems inadequate."

Donati and Donais echoed Bruno's sentiment.

Lamberti waved her right hand dismissively, saying that what she'd done was in the past and now beyond discussion. "You're here because I want to tell you how I plan to start the process of bringing this matter with Riva and Pagano to a conclusion." She gave them a summary of the incriminating evidence in the documents that Piras provided and told them what she'd given to the reporter.

"They will never go to jail. You're going to do what you previously said, desensitize the public on Riva. Nobody cares what happens to Pagano. At some point, you'll eliminate them because they pose a threat to the republic."

"You're as perceptive as I was led to believe. If you understand me, and I believe you do, then you'll know I'm not a forgiving person."

"There's just one problem."

"What is that?"

"You won't kill them until you know who murdered Carolina."

"A necessary prerequisite for which you still need to provide the answer."

"Acardi told me that Pagano killed my wife and unborn child and that you knew about it."

"That's correct. The only reason that he's alive is that I need to know if he, Riva, or a third party killed Carolina. When I find out, I'll kill that person."

"Is that why you released them from prison?" Bruno asked. "You couldn't interrogate them in the manner you intended while they were in jail."

"Precisely."

"What if I told you that Pagano didn't kill Carolina?"

"Without proof, I'd say you were lying so you can get me to stand aside while you exact your revenge. I saw the entry and exit logs for the Quirinal. Pagano and one of the Heritage Restorations crew were the only outsiders, besides Carolina, who entered the building the night she was murdered. That's how I know either Pagano, Riva, or possibly this third person murdered her. From what I know, he's a Mafia soldier. If he killed Carolina, someone gave him the order."

"What if I told you it wasn't any of those three? What if I said that the killer was Gabrielle Riva?"

"She's not on the log, and it's nearly impossible to sneak into the presidential palace."

"Nearly?"

"I'm not going there."

"According to the security officer I spoke with, ministerial family members don't have to log in or out," Bruno stated.

"That hardly makes her the killer. Her goal in life is to become the first lady. The entire country knows that."

"Did you see the police analysis of the murder weapon? The coroner attached it to the autopsy report."

"I read it. The letter opener belonged to my husband. There were no fingerprints on it."

"But there was residue," Bruno said, removing from his jacket pocket the autopsy report that Acardi gave him. Finding the relevant section, he handed it to Lamberti.

"Tree moss, citral, lilial, cinnamyl alcohol, benzyl alcohol, titanium dioxide, mica clay, green tea, and another 30 or 40 other chemicals or ingredients with which I'm not familiar. You're telling me this was on my husband's knife?"

"The handle. The killer used gloves or wiped the weapon clean of their fingerprints. However, they didn't use a chemical cleaner to remove the residue they'd left on the murder weapon."

"Meaning?"

"Meaning that the chemicals and ingredients listed in the police report are commonly used to manufacture perfume and cosmetics."

"Get to the point."

"Did you ever touch your husband's letter opener?"

"Not since the day I gave it to him."

"Did anyone else?"

"Security wouldn't allow anyone but my husband to touch it. It was a knife. A weapon."

"I believe that a woman, who probably touched her face before handling the knife, killed Carolina. Ms. Biagi was, according to the autopsy, five feet, nine inches tall. Pagano, I would guess, is five feet, five inches - or thereabouts. Gratiano Riva is a good six feet, three inches in height. According to the coroner, Ms. Biagi's throat was cut by someone between five and five feet, one inch in height. The coroner deduced this from the angle the knife made across the victim's throat."

"Gabriele Riva is that height," Lamberti said.

"If we obtain her perfume and makeup, I believe their ingredients will match the chemicals the lab found on the knife."

"Many women use the same or similar perfume and cosmetics."

"But they don't have the undocumented access to the presidential palace granted to ministerial families."

"You make a compelling case." Lamberti was silent as she contemplated what Bruno said.

"We share a need for vengeance and closure. Don't deprive me of this," Bruno pleaded.

"It's ironic. We're about to commit murder, for which we could and should be arrested and incarcerated for the rest of our lives."

"Some would consider removing cancerous growths, such as Pagano and Riva's, as a necessary surgical procedure. Sometimes the scales of justice need a counterweight," Bruno said. "That's you and, in this situation, me."

Lamberti nodded in agreement. "Pagano is yours, and the Rivas are mine."

CHAPTER 14

THE ARTICLE, DETAILING instances of corruption committed by Gratiano Riva in concert with Baldassare Pagano, was slated to run in two days in the morning edition of *la Repubblica*, the leading newspaper in Rome to which Pia Lamberti had connections. To keep the accusations from boomeranging and impaling President Orsini, the newspaper would indicate the documents came from Piras, who could hardly comment since he was dead. The paper teased this was the first of several exposés on Riva and Pagano and the tip of the iceberg on their illicit activities.

"That will get his attention," Bruno said as he handed the paper back to Lamberti. "Why will it run in two days? Why not now?" The three investigators, who were staying at the residence, were again sitting in Lamberti's office.

"I need to finish my web."

Bruno didn't understand what that meant but knew that it couldn't be good for either Pagano or Riva. "What's your next move?" he asked.

"After the article is published, I'll call Riva for a meeting. Since the newspaper states that the material for the article came from Piras, Riva will know he's backed into a corner and withdraw. After which, we'll have our reckoning."

"Have Pagano and Ricci been released?" Bruno asked.

"I'm told that Ricci is going to the residence in Tivoli, and Pagano is on his way here, just as you requested."

"I'm curious. What would you have done to Pagano if he'd been the one who killed Carolina?"

"Sliced his neck. Now that I know he didn't kill her, the manner of his death is up to you. What do you have planned? You haven't told me."

Bruno ignored the question. "I want answers from Pagano before he dies, but I need to be sure he's telling me the truth because I have only one shot at this."

"And your questions?"

"Why he targeted my wife and saved the letter that I wrote her."

"And how do you plan to ensure he's truthful?"

"I thought you could help."

"I can."

Baldassare Pagano and Romelo Ricci were taken from their cells without explanation and brought to the parking garage. Ricci was told he was being set free, and Pagano that he was going elsewhere. The Mafia chieftain ordered his lieutenant to go to his house in Tivoli and keep a low profile. If he didn't hear from him in two days, he was on his own.

Ricci was handcuffed, placed in the backseat of a car with a guard beside him, and a black canvas bag thrown over his head. After being driven to a taxi stand in the middle of the city, the guard removed his handcuffs and handed him his wallet and other personal possessions confiscated on his arrest. Throwing open the door to the vehicle, he told Ricci to get out.

Similarly, Pagano was handcuffed and buckled into the back seat of an SUV, and a black canvas bag thrown over his head. Zunino was at the wheel with Silvio Villa, Pia Lamberti's number two enforcer, beside him. Villa stood six feet, two inches tall, and was 300 pounds of sculpted muscle with a neck like a tree trunk.

Zunino drove to Pia Lamberti's residence and parked at the rear of the mansion. He and Villa then unbuckled Pagano and guided the mafioso through the back door and down a set of stairs to the basement.

The basement was large, and its concrete floors and walls were unpainted. In the far-right corner was a bathroom. A sizeable commercial incinerator was in the center, which Lamberti used to destroy copies of classified documents along with anything else that needed to be reduced to ash, which occasionally included bodies. Twenty feet in front of the incinerator and next to a floor drain was a metal chair. Four flex cuffs were on the floor behind it.

After shoving Pagano into the chair, they removed his handcuffs and replaced them with the flex cuffs, binding his limbs to the chair. Once secured, they pulled his hood.

Lamberti told Bruno that she would orchestrate a setting where Pagano would feel powerless and afraid of being killed. She ordered that the incinerator be set at its maximum setting, which produced a wild vortex of flames within it and threw off a lot of heat. That seemed to have the desired effect on Pagano - transfixed by the intertwining flames. The emanating heat caused sweat to drip from his forehead and down his face.

The basement was well lit but not bright. Zunino and Villa placed two 3,200 lumen LED industrial lights on tripods at 45-degree angles to the left and right of the mafioso so that they shone directly on his face and caused him to squint. They then retrieved a dozen plastic water containers, each one gallon in size, which were against the wall to their right, placing them and a towel on the floor beside Pagano.

"Remember me?" Bruno asked as he came from behind the mafioso, eventually taking a position five feet in front of him.

"I should have killed you," Pagano replied, the scorn he felt for Bruno evident in his voice as he squinted at him.

"I'll take that as a yes. Here's how this is going to work. I'm going to ask you several questions. However, I can't trust a snake like you to answer truthfully because I believe you'd enjoy lying to me. Therefore, I'm going to show you what happens if I suspect you're lying."

Bruno nodded. Villa, standing behind Pagano's chair, tilted it back against his midsection and placed the towel over the mafioso's face, holding onto it with both hands. Pagano, now finding it difficult to breathe, panicked and started gasping for air. Zunino uncapped a plastic container and was about to pour water over the towel when Bruno held up his hand, momentarily stopping him.

"You're going to be waterboarded. There's nothing you can do to stop that. Breathing will become extremely difficult once water saturates the towel. The towel acts as a one-way valve - it lets water into your mouth and nose but not out through the cloth. A demonstration."

Bruno nodded to Zunino, who slowly poured water over the towel for the next 16 seconds. The mafioso bucked as his body sensed he was drowning. Once the container was empty, Villa removed the towel and tipped the chair forward until it rested on four legs. Pagano coughed, spit out water, and took great gasps of air into his lungs.

"One more time to illustrate what will happen if I suspect you're lying." As they were repeating the process, and Villa was securing the wet towel over Pagano's face and tilting the chair back, the mafioso tried to tip it to the side. Villa was extremely strong. The chair didn't budge, and the waterboarding went unabated. Afterward, Pagano again threw up water and gasped for air, his recovery taking twice as long as before.

"Did you kill my wife and unborn child?"

Pagano's eyes involuntarily darted from side to side, indicating that he was thinking about how to answer the question. Once he saw Zunino pick up another container of water, he admitted he did.

"Why?"

Pagano explained he was having dinner with Riva at a restaurant near the train station in Milan when he saw the look of recognition in the eyes of a uniformed female officer. "The commission spent a small fortune grooming Riva for higher office within the government, even having some of his rivals disappear or have incapacitating accidents. I was afraid your wife would destroy years of planning and investment if she reported seeing him with us."

"You were at the table in the private alcove?"

Pagano confirmed he was.

"I was new to the force. I don't remember your face, but I remember that night. My wife recognized everyone at the table except for Riva," Bruno said.

"Unemotionally, put yourself in my shoes. Would you have taken that chance?"

"Tell me exactly how she died."

"It was so long ago; it's difficult at my age to remember."

"Let me help your recall."

This time the waterboarding lasted 25 seconds, and Pagano, who was 70 years old, looked like he was about to have a heart attack, finding it difficult to regain his breath. Zunino whispered in Bruno's ear he needed to go slower, or he'd be interrogating a corpse.

Undeterred, Bruno asked again. This time, Pagano's memory was perfect.

"I'm curious why you kept, for nearly 25 years, the letter I wrote my wife."

Pagano laughed.

"What's so funny?"

"The irony. Saving that letter was unintentional. It was an oversight. I wanted your wife to die in what would look like a robbery. To make it believable, we took whatever we thought was valuable. Since we wanted to leave quickly, Ricci threw whatever was on the desk into a pillowcase. He never looked at what he took."

"Taking the letter was unintentional?"

"Yes."

"Why keep it for 25 years?"

"We forgot about it and everything else taken from your apartment. Ricci worked for the Acconci family, so he was staying in Trieste, which is near Venice. I was returning to Rome and didn't want to have anything in my possession that connected me to the murder. Therefore, he took what we stole and hid it in the basement of his home. When Armino Acconci died, his son Lazzaro succeeded him. I offered Ricci a position as my lieutenant. As chairperson of the commission, Lazzaro couldn't object. Ricci moved to Rome."

"And everyone forgot about what he'd hidden."

"Until an article that mentioned you brought down Rodolfo Rizzo. That triggered Ricci's memory. He returned to

Trieste, broke into his old house, retrieved what he'd hidden, and brought it to Tivoli. I read the letter and came up with a plan to lure you to Rome."

"To kill me."

Pagano didn't respond because the answer was obvious.

"Why? I'm no longer in the Polizia di Stato."

"Revenge. You caused the death of Rodolfo Rizzo and cost the commission a great deal of money because his bank was the primary source for laundering our illicit cash flow. It wasn't just me who wanted your head on a platter; every member of the commission wanted you killed because you cost them millions."

"How did you know I'd fall for your plan?"

"You would have walked over broken glass or hot coals to get the name of your wife's killer. Who wouldn't? As it turned out, I didn't need a plan to get you to Rome. Fate intervened and brought you here."

"Watch him," Bruno suddenly said to Zunino and Villa. "I'm going upstairs." Bruno ascended the interior staircase to the second floor, where he found Donati and Donais having an espresso with Lamberti.

"Did you find out what you needed to know?" she asked. Bruno said he did.

"Do you want me to take care of him for you?"

"You won't have to. Can you come downstairs and bring your cell phone with you? I need a photo."

"This should be interesting." Lamberti grabbed her cell phone off her lap. Donati and Donati followed them to the basement.

As soon as Pagano saw her, his expression changed from one of arrogance, the attitude that he'd last exhibited to Bruno, to fear.

"Now what?" Lamberti asked Bruno out of earshot of Pagano.

"Cut his bonds and let him dry off and comb his hair. I want a photo of him kissing your hand."

"You're joking. You never explained to me how you planned to kill him. Now would be a good time."

Bruno explained and told her what she needed to tell Pagano.

"I'd put a bullet in his head, find Ricci and do the same, and be done with it. But it's your call."

Lamberti ordered Pagano cut loose and told him he could dry off in the bathroom. Villa pointed out its location and accompanied him, holding the door open to monitor what he was doing. When they returned, Pagano looked presentable, at least from a distance.

Lamberti unlocked her phone and handed it to Bruno. "Come with me," she told Pagano.

With Zunino and Villa on either side of him, he followed her outside. Bruno, Donati, and Donais brought up the rear. They walked onto the spread of grass behind the residence, where Lamberti turned and faced the mafioso.

"Kiss my hand," she said.

Pagano, who was intimidated by Lamberti, complied without hesitation. Bruno took the photo.

"You've just retired from the family business. This isn't a request; it's a statement of fact. If you refuse, I'll have you thrown into the incinerator in my basement."

"There's no such thing as retirement from the family. It doesn't exist because trust wrapped in fear binds us together. Nobody leaves the game. If I announce my retirement, I might as well schedule my funeral at the same time."

"If you refuse, you won't have time to plan your funeral. We'll hold it in less than a minute. Lamberti's mind seemed to drift. Stay here," she said as she went to where Bruno, Donati, and Donati were standing. Zunino and Villa stayed with Pagano.

"Come with me," she told Bruno, before walking to a bench 20 paces away and sitting. Bruno sat and returned her phone.

"You said you wanted to make Pagano suffer by making the commission believe he made a deal with me to stay out of prison - borne out because he and Ricci are out of jail and solidified by the photo you took of Pagano kissing my hand. That makes it a certainty that he'll be hunted until a contract killer puts him out of his misery."

"That's my plan."

"You realize dead is dead. Neither Pagano nor Ricci will return to the living and look at a replay of their deaths and say *well-played*."

"You're stating the obvious."

"Your plan is clumsy but has merit. I have an alternative that will make him, and Ricci suffer. I assume you're including his lieutenant in your plan?"

Bruno said he was.

"What I have planned will guarantee their deaths and, in the end, give you far more satisfaction."

"Your alternative?"

She told him, saying that in return for her help, Pagano needed to tell her everything about the commission and the business activities of the five families. "Acting on that information will put the Italian Mafia back on its heels. As a former law enforcement officer, I don't have to tell you the number of lives that would save or the misery it would curtail."

"I like it. My plan was clumsy."

Lamberti returned to Pagano.

"I'm letting you go," Lamberti said.

"Have Bruno put a bullet in me. Once that photo gets out, I'm a dead man. He won't have a problem pulling the trigger. After all, I killed his wife and unborn child in cold blood and have no regrets about it."

Although Bruno's face displayed a lack of emotion, something he'd learned over the years to piss off perps who would try to provoke him into striking them so they could get their cases tossed or have him thrown in a cell for beating the crap out of them, he was seething inside.

"He doesn't decide life and death; I do," Lamberti said, taking control. "He's agreed to let you live if you detail the activities of the five families and the commission."

"I'm not a ratto."

"To be accurate, you're lower than a rat, so spare me the false shield of nobility. You'd betray anyone if it was to your benefit and could get away with it. The terms of our deal will be you tell me all you know about the commission and the five families, and provide actionable information on corrupt officials, money laundering, smuggling routes, and so forth. In return, I give you my word that your anonymity, along with that of your lieutenant, will be guaranteed forever."

"I saw Bruno taking a photo of us. What was that about?"

"I plan to send it to every member of the commission. Therefore, you accept my offer, or you're dead."

"They'll find me in Italy. I'll need to leave the country."

"Where do you want to go?"

"Casablanca, Morocco."

"I'm sure this wasn't a spur-of-the-moment thought. Why there?"

"I have my reasons."

"Morocco has no extradition with Italy."

"That's one."

"Done. I'll issue you and Ricci passports with new identities, along with birth certificates and other documentation necessary to facilitate your anonymity. I'll also have a charter aircraft transport you both to a private terminal that doesn't have a facial recognition program. Someone will meet you in Casablanca and escort you to your new home."

"It's well-known that you're treacherous, but always keep your word."

"Yes, the witch always keeps her word."

Pagano cleared his throat, knowing that she was referring to herself by the nickname he'd given her, which others had subsequently adopted. "We have a deal," he said.

"Let's go inside and start our debriefing."

"Now? Detailing what I know will take us through the night and possibly the next."

"I'm an insomniac."

CHAPTER 15

FOUR OF THE five Mafia families comprising the commission met in Palermo at the home of Carmine Soldati, the chief mafioso in Sicily. Soldati was rail-thin, six-foot, one inch tall with a gaunt face and thinning brown hair that was being outnumbered by an encroaching horde of gray. Balding in the front, he combed his hair to the right to conceal as much of his scalp as he could. As the second longest-serving commission member next to Pagano, the chairmanship automatically fell to him once Pagano could no longer function as chairman. The other members regarded him as a "cold fish," meaning they believed he was aloof and lacked emotion or any semblance of humanness - which was correct in every respect.

Soldati began, as custom dictated, by summarizing the commission's business ventures, some of which were legal and some not. They discussed Heritage Restorations, concluding that with Piras's death and Pagano's arrest, the writing was on the wall that the government would soon exclude Heritage from bidding for government contracts. All agreed this necessitated they buy an existing Italian restoration company and replace its management with family members. Soldati would oversee these efforts. The second item on the agenda was starting the process to select a fifth family to run the territory formerly under Pagano's purview. Since he had no blood relatives, because they were killed in feuds and vendettas over the years, each member could nominate a family to replace him at the table. Once put forward, tradition dictated the chair make the final decision. The last item for discussion was Pagano, each family having received a photo of him kissing Pia Lamberti's hand. Based on this, and that he and Ricci were out of prison and back in Tivoli, the belief was that he was cooperating with authorities. With the solution on how to protect the families unanimous, Soldati called the arbitrator.

Vespa was 100 percent successful in arbitrating the commission's previous problems. Recruited by Pagano, he was the only person to have seen or spoken to the arbitrator. The consensus among family members, because of the ruthless efficiency of the kills, was that Vespa was ex-military. Although the commission had the assassin's contact number, which changed constantly, and wiring instructions to their offshore bank account, Pagano was the only person who interfaced with Vespa. Therefore, the call from Soldati came as a shock to both. It surprised the arbitrator that the commission put Pagano and Ricci under contract for €100,000 per head, and it stunned Soldati that Vespa was a woman.

"It's surprising to see a woman in your line of work. It must be an advantage in getting close to your victims."

"Occasionally. Where are the targets?" Vespa asked, getting down to business.

"At Pagano's Tivoli residence. Do you know where that is?"

"Yes."

"Assume they won't be there long. They'll suspect the commission has ordered their deaths and will attempt to leave the country."

"I'll arbitrate. Wire the money," she said, ending the call.

Vespa used four weapons to fulfill her contracts - an Accuracy International rifle with scope, an AR-15 rifle capable of full-automatic fire, a Sig Sauer P320 pistol, and an Ari B' Lilah knife, a favorite of Israeli counter-terrorism units. These, along with an ample amount of ammo, were stored in a hidden compartment within the trunk of her vehicle.

Having been to Pagano's Tivoli residence and knowing the area was hilly with dense brush and trees, she formulated a plan that would take advantage of the topography and seasonal dryness. Driving to several hardware stores, she accumulated a dozen plastic gas cans, paying for them in cash and filling them at various gas stations between Rome, where she lived, and Tivoli.

As she entered Tivoli, she turned off the highway and onto a dirt road that meandered through the hills, eventually stopping the car atop a hill that gave her a view of Pagano's residence. Getting out of the vehicle, she tore a small leaf from a plant beside the road and tossed it into the air. Using it to gauge the direction of the wind, she watched as it veered 30 degrees to her right. Getting back in the car, she drove 50 yards back up the road to another spot which also gave her a similar view of Pagano's home. She again tore a leaf off a plant and tossed it in the air. This time, it floated directly away from her. She was downwind from the house.

Vespa planned to drench the surrounding brush and base of trees on the hill with gas, light it, and create a fire. She would then relocate to an upwind position since anyone trying to escape the blaze, by foot or vehicle, would flee in a direction opposite the fire. This would make it easy to dispatch her targets. Taking two of the containers from the rear of her vehicle, she walked down the hill, pouring gasoline on the tinder-dry grass and the bottom of the cedar trees until the containers were empty. It took five additional trips to empty the 12 containers. Once the hillside was soaked, she lit her Zippo lighter and touched it to the grass. The fire started slowly, picking up momentum and ferocity as the wind grabbed the flames. She then got in her vehicle and, taking the dirt road to the opposite side of the house, found a spot on a hill that gave her an unobstructed view of the residence and driveway.

Pagano and Ricci were in the study when a guard rushed in and said there was a fire in the hills and that it was coming towards them.

"It's time," Pagano said to Ricci. "Tell the men you selected to bring the vehicle to the front of the residence."

Ricci went to relay the message.

As the two men, who had near-identical physiques to Ricci and Pagano, pulled the vehicle in front of the house and got out, neither felt nor heard the rounds that went through their faces, all but obliterating them - Vespa's signature shot. Ricci and Pagano watched through the window. Once the men were down, they approached the bodies. Removing rings and watches, along with personal items from their pockets, they planted them on the bodies.

"The fire will be here before long. The bodies will burn to a cinder, and the witch will believe they're us until the autopsies contradict that assumption. By that time, we'll be somewhere she'll never find us. She's not the only one who can obtain new identities."

"Do you hear that?" Ricci asked. The noise, which was at first almost imperceptible, was becoming increasingly loud.

Pagano shook his head, the scowl on his face showing he knew what was happening and there was nothing he could do to stop it. "It seems the witch doesn't trust us and sent sitters to ensure we're here in the morning," he said.

"What do you want to do?"

"Cut a cigar and pull up a chair. We're not going anywhere."

The 21 NOCS operatives within the Chinook were tightly strapped into their webbed seats, except for the team commander, who was standing behind the pilot and had a tight grip on the back of his seat, the aircraft jostled by the turbulence created by the fire below them.

"Quite a blaze, and it's headed straight for the house," the pilot said to the commander. "Are those the two you're supposed to watch?" he asked, pointing to the bodies next to a vehicle that was ahead and several hundred feet below them.

"I hope not. My orders are to secure the area around Baldassare Pagano's home and babysit him and Romelo Ricci until the morning."

"Where do you want me to set down?"

"Not near Pagano's residence. Let's not take a chance that whoever killed these two wants to use your aircraft for target practice. Land in the hills on the side of the house opposite the fire."

"Easier said than done. The rotor diameter on a Chinook is 60 feet, and I need a 100-foot operating diameter. There's a lot of trees in these hills."

"Find a spot, and my team will hike in from there. We'll need to secure the area to ensure it's free of shooters before we approach the bodies and verify their identities - if we beat the fire to them."

The Chinook landed on the only open plot of earth in the area where its blades wouldn't encounter a tree. Not much larger than the aircraft, the heavy rear ramp flattened the brush behind it as it lowered to the ground, allowing the team to disembark and spread out. Each wore Rokid thermal imaging glasses, which resembled ordinary sunglasses. With an attached twelve-megapixel camera on the left side, the augmented reality eyewear allowed the wearer to see the thermal signature of anyone trying to hide in the brush. However, its drawback was that if they got too close to the fire, the heat emanating from it eliminated the temperature differential necessary for the eyewear to distinguish a person's heat signature. The good news was that the glasses had an excellent communications interface which allowed team members to speak with one another.

Once his team dispersed, the team commander muted his mic to keep his conversation private from the rest of the team and called Zunino - telling him about the fire and that he saw two bodies on the ground beside a vehicle outside Pagano's house. He also said they appeared to be the same physical shape as the mafioso and his lieutenant. The conversation continued for another minute before the call ended.

Zunino repeated the conversation for Lamberti, who showed no emotion from what she heard.

"He couldn't verify that the bodies were Pagano and Ricci?" Lamberti asked.

"He won't know until his team works their way to the residence and examines the bodies. He'll send us photos. However, the fire appears to be headed for the house and may get there before them."

The expression on Lamberti's face turned hard, and her eyes narrowed. "The fire wasn't an act of nature. It was started deliberately. Either the commission is intent on Pagano's cremation, or he's up to something. We won't know which until the commander examines the bodies. In the meantime, I'll expedite fire trucks to the area so they can get the blaze under control before it reaches the house."

Once the team commander ended his call with Zunino, he unmuted his mic and checked in with his team, discovering that they'd spread out and were securing the area. He returned to the helicopter and found the pilot relaxing on one of the web seats in the back of the aircraft. Sitting next to him, he muted his mic. Both men had been on numerous missions together and were each called "grandpa" by the younger operatives - although not to their faces.

"Let me run something by you."

"Sure."

"Let's say this fire was started to destroy the bodies. With nothing but charred remains, it would take a coroner to determine their identities. By that time, if these weren't the persons they sent us to watch, Pagano and Ricci would be long gone."

"The fire may also have driven them outside to see what was happening, where they'd be in the open. The bodies could be the two that you were sent to babysit," the pilot countered.

"In that case, the shooter would be gone. What's the point of sticking around if your targets are dead? However, if the bodies are decoys, my bet is they're still in the area to see if they're burned."

"That's reasonable."

"If they're here, they're hiding in these hills since it's away from the fire and they can get a view of the bodies. That's where I'd be," the commander said.

"With us being here, they're probably hunkered down trying to avoid your team."

"That would be my guess. My men are securing the area, but the shooter could be outside that perimeter. How fast can you get airborne?"

"In less than a minute."

"Here's what I need you to do," the team commander said, explaining his plan.

The Chinook lifted off its postage-stamp size landing pad and began a concentric search pattern, looking for vehicles on the upwind side of the fire and on or near fire roads and trails. Ten minutes later, the pilot radioed the commander, using the Rokid communications frequency.

"You were right. There's a car parked to the side of an access road above the area your men are securing. I flew this beast past it and waited for several minutes before I made my turn so as not to tip our hand, but I don't know if that worked." He provided the coordinates.

The commander asked who was closest to the position pinpointed by the aircraft commander. Two operatives responded it was about a hundred yards away and above them.

"I want you both to approach with extreme caution. There's a high probability one or more shooter is hiding in that area. I want them taken alive but put a bullet in them if you need to defend yourselves."

Both men acknowledged their orders.

Vespa first heard the Chinook when it approached Pagano's house. However, when it continued past, and the sound of its engines gradually faded away, she assumed its route took it overhead and that it was on its way to one of the military bases outside Rome. She discarded that conclusion when the helicopter passed low over her. Had she not been in camouflaged attire, they might have seen her.

Not believing in coincidences, she took this as a sign that something was about to happen. Since she did what she was paid to do, she decided not to wait and see if the fire consumed the bodies and began putting her rifle back in its case. Pagano and Ricci were on their own. She'd done her part in keeping them alive in return for a massive payment to her offshore account. She was now retired, not wanting to press her luck in a profession where retirement usually meant getting caught or killed.

However, those plans changed abruptly when she heard an authoritative voice ordering her to drop her rifle case and interlace her fingers atop her head. She obeyed. Several seconds later, a second voice, this one coming from her right, ordered her to turn around. She did and saw two men in combat gear. Both had the red dot from their MP5 submachine gun on her torso.

When the team commander arrived, Vespa had her hands bound behind her back, and her ankles were also zip-tied.

Recognizing the person lying on the ground, the commander broke into a smile. "Good evening, Mrs. Riva. I know someone who will want to have a long chat with you."

The team commander walked to a spot where no one could hear him, muted his mic, and called Zunino, who instructed him on how to handle Gabriele Riva. He returned to his prisoner.

"Gag her, throw a bag over her head, and take her to the aircraft," the commander said to the two men who'd captured Vespa. "One more thing. Whoever you two think this is - it isn't."

The two men, who were veterans with over a decade of military service each, were used to such orders. "You mean this guy on the ground?" one asked, eliciting a smile from his commander.

As firetrucks raced into the area, all but the two members of the NOCS team that had Vespa in custody at the helicopter assembled at the house. The commander, looking at the faceless bodies beside the car, didn't know if they were Pagano and Ricci. That question resolved itself when he entered the house and came face-to-face with them. He informed Lamberti.

"Hand your phone to Pagano," Lamberti told the commander, who was familiar with both him and Ricci since his team captured them in Guidonia.

He handed his phone to Pagano, who reluctantly took it.

"You've been ignoring my calls," Lamberti said.

He didn't respond. There was nothing to say.

Lamberti continued after the pause. "We caught the person who killed your men, and I plan to have a long conversation with her this evening. Tell me what you know about Gabriele Riva. Leave anything out, and our deal is off."

That got Pagano talking. For the next 20 minutes, he gave her chapter and verse on Oriana Vespa, also known as Gabriele Riva. "Let's not play games," Pagano said once he'd given Lamberti what she wanted. "You and I both know what I tried to do. You said you'd go through with our deal if I told you about Gabriele. Are Ricci and I still going to Morocco in the morning?"

"My word is inviolate, and our deal stands. You and your lieutenant will have your new documentation and leave for Casablanca, Morocco, tomorrow morning. Until then, I'll have the special forces team protect you both from, shall we say, other unforeseen happenstances."

CHAPTER 16

WHEN THE CHINOOK returned to Spinaceto, the two operatives who accompanied Gabriele Riva cut her leg restraints and escorted her off the aircraft to a car, beside which Zunino and Villa were waiting. Driven to Pia Lamberti's residence and taken to the basement, they tied her to a chair in the center of the room and removed her hood and gag. Squinting in the face of two LED lights which were in front and on both sides of her, she saw her husband was similarly bound to a metal chair to her right.

Told by Zunino not to speak to one another, they waited in silence. Several minutes later, Lamberti came down the interior stairway followed by the three investigators. In her right hand, she carried a folded newspaper.

"Oriana Vespa," Lamberti said. "Or should I say, Mrs. Gabriele Riva?"

"Are you insane? My husband is a minister and presidential candidate. You must let us go."

Gratiano Riva remained silent, familiar with the immense power of the country's intelligence czar.

"I'm not releasing a hired assassin for the Mafia," Lamberti answered.

Vespa, who gave her a defiant look, didn't respond.

"I had an interesting conversation with Baldassare Pagano. He told me about you and your husband."

"I don't believe you."

"You were born in Sermoneta, a small town 50 miles south of Rome. You were an only child whose father left your mother just after you were born. Pagano came to your town to collect on a debt, met you when you were 17, and had his way with you. Your mother, who knew of your relationship with him, died a year later of an unknown ailment. He taught you how to shoot. You proved to be a natural and became an expert marksperson. Your lover took advantage of that talent and your loyalty to him by using you as a contract killer for the commission. You continued to accept these contracts after your marriage to Gratiano, which Pagano arranged."

"Baldassare Pagano would say anything to save his hide."

"Normally, I'd agree with you. However, I've incentivized him to tell the truth."

"It will be the word of a career criminal against the wife of a presidential candidate with a lifetime of service to the country."

"Let's talk about that lifetime of service. This is tomorrow's edition of *la Repubblica*, which will document your husband's corruption." Lamberti unfolded the paper she was carrying and held it between the couple, partially shielding them from the LED lights and allowing them to see the banner heading: *Riva Corruption.*

A typical newspaper article ranges from 200 to 500 words, with the latter consuming between 12.5 and 14.25 column inches, which is how editors quantify length. The article on Riva's corruption was nearly 28 inches. Lamberti finished reading aloud the first paragraph when she looked up to see that Gratiano Riva appeared to be in shock - his mouth gaping open, and his eyes glazed over. Gabriele looked pissed.

"The question is: what do I do with a corrupt politician and a contract killer?" Lamberti asked.

"My husband will claim the president fabricated this to discredit him before the election. As to my weapons, since I always wear gloves, there won't be any fingerprints on them. I'll say they aren't mine. Who will believe that a homemaker is an assassin? That accusation reeks of desperation. Set us free, and we'll forget about this kidnapping and won't have you arrested. If not, my husband will have you thrown in jail."

Gratiano Riva looked at his wife as if she'd grabbed a rattlesnake by the tail but ignored the head - the business part of the serpent which contained the fangs and venom.

"Do you know who I am? Do you know what I do?"

"You're the witch."

"A description I've grown to like. I want to clarify that you're not here because of your husband's massive corruption or that you're a brazen killer. You're here because I want to know why you murdered Carolina Bragi," Lamberti said, stepping forward until she again stood two feet in front of the couple.

"My mistress?" Gratiano responded with a note of incredulity. "Is that what this is about? Who cares? She was a woman for hire, a pleasure vehicle, a toy - nothing more. We both profited from the relationship. She got a lavish lifestyle and some money, while I got what older men want from attractive young women."

"Wrong answer," Lamberti responded in a menacing tone. "She was an intelligent lady who devoted her life to protecting this country from people such as you and your wife. Carolina didn't deserve to die, and she wasn't a toy to be discarded at will. She was a government agent who worked for me."

That statement seemed to stun the Riva's, who each displayed a look of disbelief.

"To be clear, when I asked why you killed Carolina Biagi, I wasn't asking you," Lamberti said, staring Gratiano Riva in the eye. "I was asking your wife," she intoned, shifting her gaze to Gabriele.

"Another baseless accusation without proof," Vespa replied.

"The coroner discovered makeup on the handle of the murder weapon. I'm certain that it will match yours," Lamberti said.

Extending her arm towards Zunino, he handed her the murder weapon, its handle wrapped in a cloth secured with duct tape.

"The coroner estimated the height of the killer by calculating the angle of the blade across Carolina's throat. He put that height at between five feet and five feet, one inch. While this eliminates your husband as the murderer, it doesn't exclude you."

"Many people are my height. I also suspect that makeup is common to most women and even some men. Everything you have is circumstantial. There's no proof - only allegations."

"You had access to the Quirinal at the time of her death."

"So did many others. As much as you would like to frame me for her murder, ask yourself why I would kill Ms. Biagi? Look at my husband," Gabriele said. "He's quite handsome and has the wandering eye of most men. Over our nearly 20 years of marriage, he's had several mistresses. Although I've met none of them, Gratiano has shown me their photos and described their sexual exploits. I get off on hearing it and picturing him with them. I can handle the infidelity and, oddly, embrace it."

"Then why did you kill her?"

"Let's say, hypothetically, that I did - although I'm not admitting it. Killing her wouldn't have been about jealousy or insecurity. It would have been to protect my husband's career. When that nosy bitch went beyond screwing him and eavesdropped on his conversations, whose revelations could have cost him his position at the ministry and his rise to the presidency, something had to be done," Gabriele growled.

"And the arbitrator killed her?" Lamberti asked, using the term for Vespa that Pagano had given her.

"The arbitrator doesn't decide who lives or dies - I carry out the sentence."

"I see where this is going. It won't be possible to convince a judge or jury beyond a reasonable doubt, and possibly the public, that Gabriele Riva is Oriana Vespa, a contract killer for the Mafia who murdered Carolina Biagi," Lamberti said as she walked behind the Rivas. "No one will believe anything that Baldassare Pagano says to corroborate these allegations because he's a career criminal and a known liar. I believe you both will come up with a creative story for every allegation. Whether they will blame President Orsini for the *la Repubblica* article - that's a flip of the coin. Although the evidence against you is solid, an investigation into the allegations wouldn't conclude until after the election. If you ascend to the presidency, these allegations will disappear."

"With the *la Repubblica* article, you've unwittingly catapulted me into the presidency."

"I do nothing unwittingly, and you won't have that opportunity."

Lamberti, standing behind Gratiano Riva, leaned forward and sliced his throat from end to end. She then took two steps to her left and did the same to Gabriele Riva.

"Clean the knife, put it back in the evidence bag, and give it to Acardi," Lamberti said, handing it to Zunino. "Tell him he can return it to the police evidence room."

"Do you still want me to dispose of the bodies as we discussed?"

"Yes. Use the heat gun to seal the shrink wrap. I don't want air getting to them. Do you have the combination?" Lamberti asked.

Zunino confirmed he memorized it and the entry instructions that she'd given him. Nodding to Villa, they left to get what they needed to shrink wrap the bodies.

The tunnel was constructed a century ago. Burrowed deep into the hill on which the Quirinal sat, it provided the president of the republic with an emergency escape route and a way to exit the palace without being seen. One end was behind a panel in the president's bathroom, while the other was inside a large monument within a park a mile away. Officially, only the president, the head of his security detail, and the intelligence czar knew its existence. DeRosa and the several members of the maintenance and engineering staff charged with maintaining it also knew.

The park entrance was at the bottom of a 15-foot-high sign which proclaimed the name of the park. The first six of that 15 feet was a steel base, which was unseen from a distance because a wall of tall plants surrounded it. Zunino forced his way into the tall plantings with Gabriele Riva atop his shoulders. Behind him, Villa followed with Gratiano Riva. They did their best to keep from breaking the stems and branches of the plants. Mostly, they succeeded - although not completely.

When they got to the steel base, they found a one-foot-wide dirt perimeter maintained around the sign base. Placing the plastic-sheeted body on the dirt, Zunino went to the spot on the steel wall where Lamberti told him there would be a recessed keypad, cautioning it wouldn't be visible. Pressing where she told him, he heard a click. A keypad, which was an enhancement made over the last century, popped out. Entering the ten-digit code he'd memorized; a section of the steel base opened and revealed a doorway. Once the lighting within the tunnel activated, they saw a 10-feet-wide and seven-foot-high downward sloping concrete walkway within.

Zunino and Villa, slinging the Rivas over their shoulders, entered the tunnel. Villa, the last one through, shoved the door closed.

It was a mile to the president's office, the first quarter of which was downhill. The rest was flat. At the end of the tunnel, a ladder extended 25 feet above them - presumably to the president's bathroom.

"This is going to suck," Zunino said as he readjusted the body on his shoulder and climbed. Villa, who was in spectacular shape and had the heavier body, didn't comment or break a sweat as he ascended.

The ladder ended at a three-by-three-foot door that opened upwards and to the left. Zunino squeezed his way through and stepped into a lighted space that was square and five feet on a side. Opposite him was a handle attached to a piece of elegant wood, the top and bottom of which were in a grooved track. Pulling the panel aside, he entered the president's bathroom. Villa followed.

After laying both bodies on the floor, they reversed the route they'd taken and exited the tunnel. Returning to Lamberti's residence, they went to her office and found her sitting in her chair, with the investigators on the sofa beside her.

"It went as planned," Zunino said.

"You both did well. Get some rest. You and Silvio need to be back at the Quirinal at six in the morning to finish things up."

"Understood."

Zunino and Villa arrived at the presidential palace at precisely 6 a.m. and went to the security counter. Their names were on the access log, and they were each issued a pass that would allow them entry to the president's office. After placing what they had in their pockets on a tray that went through an x-ray machine, they walked through a body scanner and received clearance to enter the building.

Their ruse was that they were installing a highly classified security system. Orsini, who Lamberti kept informed on what occurred since the three investigators arrived in Rome, supported her previous actions and what she was about to do. He directed building security to allow Zunino and Villa to work unsupervised and undisturbed. He also directed that the guard outside his office remain off-station until noon due to the installation of the security device. No one knew why this was necessary since the device was within the president's office and out of sight of the guard, but they weren't about to question the president of the republic. As cover, Orsini left Rome for the day and campaigned outside the city.

Zunino and Villa saw that the ladders, tools, and materials required for their job were neatly stacked in the hall. Using the security code given him by Lamberti, Zunino tapped in the numbers, and he and Villa entered the president's office.

They began by placing drop cloths over the furniture and on the floors, using the tall ladder to wrap the Murano chandelier in plastic. They next removed the framed paintings and mirrors, stacked them to the side, and covered them with plastic. The prep work took 90 minutes. Once this was complete, they hauled the Rivas out of the bathroom and laid them on the office floor.

Referring to Zunino and Villa as contractors was inaccurate. Even the moniker of handypersons was a stretch. Lamberti understood their limitations and told DeRosa that, since there was already a large opening in President Orsini's wall, she moved up installing an anti-eavesdropping device that was to be placed within that space. Her intel people would install it, but his staff would have to smooth the wall and paper it afterward. DeRosa was okay with that arrangement and scheduled his men to begin their handiwork at noon.

The original crack within the president's wall was three inches wide and ran from floor to ceiling. The person attempting to repair that crack widened it with a saber saw, after which he discovered the body. Subsequently, to see what else might be hidden, the opening became the entire wall - which was more than enough space to accommodate the Rivas.

Villa hoisted the bodies into the space as Zunino cut quarter sheets of the half-inch plywood and stacked them within the opening. As Villa held each of the Rivas up, his partner nailed plywood between the wall supports and encircled the couple - creating a floor-to-ceiling enclosure that would hide the bodies, should anyone cut into the wall in the future. They finished by sealing the opening with drywall, followed by taping and mudding it - meaning they applied fiberglass tape over the seams and covered it and the screw holes with three coats of drywall compound. After it dried, they sanded the area to create a smooth surface. It wasn't close to the work expected from a general contractor, but it was good enough so that DeRosa's crew would only have to deal with cosmetics rather than rip the wall open again and replace the drywall.

At 8:30 a.m., Zunino and Villa brought their tools and unused construction materials, along with several garbage bags containing the remnants of the sheeting, and placed them atop the unused materials outside the president's office. DeRosa said that he would take it away once he and his men finished.

Returning to Lamberti's residence, Zunino and Villa were in time to join her and the three investigators for a late breakfast, during which they updated everyone on their handiwork.

"How are you going to explain the Riva's disappearance?" Bruno asked Lamberti.

"I'll have the Polizia di Stato issue a warrant for Gratiano Riva's arrest on charges of corruption and send officers to his home to serve it. They'll find a computer-printed letter of apology, confessing his misdeeds and so forth, and a statement that he and his wife are already out of the country. It will be on ministry letterhead."

"That only leaves Pagano and Ricci," Bruno said.

"Are you ready?"

"After 25 years, what do you think?"

CHAPTER 17

P IA LAMBERTI'S RANGE Rover passed through the gates of
Baldassare Pagano's residence, the smell of smoke still
in the air from the extinguished blaze which, judging
from the blackened ground in front of the house, came within
100 yards of destroying it. Zunino parked the vehicle near
the front door and followed Lamberti, Bruno, Donati, and
Donais. Pagano and Ricci were in the study.

"Don't knock, come right in," Pagano, who was seated
behind his desk, with Ricci in a chair to his left, said upon
seeing the witch and her entourage. "Did you kill Vespa?"

"She and her husband are both dead."

Pagano and Ricci, who rarely displayed emotion, looked
worried.

"But our deal is still intact? I gave you everything you
asked for," Pagano stated, coming out not as a statement but
as an imploration.

"I always keep my word."

"And you'll fly us to Morocco?"

"Casablanca, as promised."

"We're ready. It looks like you won't be allowed to put a
bullet in me," Pagano said, giving Bruno a smug smile.

"Mauro, I'll let you and your associates finish up here and ensure they get to Casablanca. Come to my residence when you get back." She and Zunino left the room.

"Don't tell me you're our escorts to the airport?" Pagano asked with a smirk.

"To Morocco. I'm to make sure that you get there."

"The irony. The person whose wife and child I killed escorts me out of the country to start a new life. Do you realize Casablanca isn't my ultimate destination? I'll leave for someplace where you'll never find me."

"Our transport will be here in five or ten minutes," Bruno said, ignoring Pagano's taunts. Donati and Donais were silent.

"You hate me, don't you?" Pagano asked with a note of glee in his voice, trying to provoke a response.

"Intensely. You robbed me of the joy of a wife and family. I have only so much time on this earth, and I'll never be able to fill the void you've created in my life."

Pagano was about to respond when there was the sound of vehicles on the gravel drive. Ricci left the study and looked through a window that faced the front of the residence, seeing an ambulance and a Range Rover Defender pull in front of the house. Ricci told Pagano what he saw.

"An ambulance. It's a clever way to avoid the scrutiny of my former associates, who will probably have the airports staked out."

"It's time to leave," Bruno said. Pagano and Ricci followed him and the other two investigators out the front door. Villa, who was driving the Defender, was helping Dante Acardi out of the passenger side of the vehicle.

With his arm in a sling, the deputy commissioner joined the three investigators, who positioned themselves ten feet to the left of Pagano and Ricci.

Pagano noticed that the ambulance driver opened the twin doors at the rear of his vehicle and removed two gurneys. "What is this?" he asked, becoming suspicious and reaching for the gun that was in the small of his back. Ricci put his left hand under his coat and was also about to withdraw his weapon.

"I wouldn't," Villa said in a stern voice.

Pagano and Ricci turned towards him. Both removed their hand from their weapon when they saw Villa looking through the sights of an AR-15 rifle, having taken it from the vehicle when Pagano was scrutinizing the ambulance. They raised their hands.

"The witch gave her word she'd fly us to Casablanca," Pagano said.

"That's still the plan. She always keeps her word," Bruno replied as he withdrew a Beretta 92FS from his shoulder holster. "She picked out the urns in which you'll be transported," he said, just before putting a bullet in Pagano's forehead. Villa put two into Ricci's heart.

The ambulance driver, one of Lamberti's guards, hoisted the bodies onto the gurneys with Villa's help and placed them inside the vehicle.

The ambulance led the way to the crematorium, with the trio and Acardi joining Villa in the Defender. Five hours after the cremation, the ashes were cool enough to be placed in separate urns. Lamberti selected them, having one engraved *Stronzo One* and the other *Stronzo Two*, stronzo the Italian equivalent of scumbag. Bruno carried Pagano's urn to the vehicle while Acardi brought Ricci. They got back into the Defender and went to the Ciampino airport.

The Gulfstream G550 arrived at the Mohammed V International Airport in Casablanca three hours after leaving Rome. Once Acardi and the trio cleared customs and immigration, an intelligence agent from the Italian consulate met them. She handed Bruno the key to a Nissan SUV. "Per Senora Lamberti's request, I loaded your destination into the navigation system. It's the only one listed. When you finish using the vehicle, return it here and call me," she said, handing him her card. "Leave the key under the mat and erase the destination."

Bruno said he understood.

The intelligence agent went onto say that the security guard at their destination was expecting their arrival and would escort them to the requested spot within the complex. "He doesn't speak Italian or English, but he knows what to do. The facility will appear deserted because the government official in charge of it has given the employees the morning off. Tell Senora Lamberti that he's thrilled with his Mercedes." She then turned around and left.

The 21-mile drive to the Sidi Othmane Abattoir Wastewater Treatment Plant took 34 minutes. As promised, the guard was expecting their arrival and escorted them to a large circular sedimentation tank, which had a railed steel platform extending halfway across it. He then left without saying a word.

The sedimentation tank, which was open at the top, removed suspended particles from wastewater. As these particles settled to the bottom, scrapers removed the sludge before releasing the water into the sewer.

Bruno carried Pagano's urn onto the platform while Acardi carried Ricci. Donati and Donais watched from a distance. Bruno went to the end of the platform while Acardi, sensing that his friend needed space, positioned himself 20 feet away.

Bruno took a deep breath and began speaking to his late wife in a loving voice. "I'm sorry I wasn't there to protect you and our child, my love, and that we weren't able to grow old together," Bruno said, as tears ran down the side of his face. "There's not a day that I haven't thought about you, nor regretted not walking you home the night you were both killed. Please forgive me. You were my sunshine and the love of my life, and I'd gladly trade the rest of it for one more day with you. Know that the person who robbed us of so much happiness can no longer enjoy another day of his life. I love you." He then opened the urn and removed the clear plastic bag, which contained several pounds of gray ash. Acardi was doing the same.

Bruno opened the bag, held it over the fetid water, and dumped Pagano's ashes into it. "While my wife and child are with the angels, I hope Satan himself pulls your soul into the deepest filth of hell." He threw the empty bag and urn into the tank. Acardi, watching Bruno, did the same.

"Your wife would be proud of you," Acardi said as Bruno joined him on his way off the platform.

"I'm not sure she'd approve of me murdering someone in cold blood."

"She'd be proud you didn't allow this evil person to destroy more lives."

Bruno put his right arm over his friend's shoulder, and they walked off the platform.

As Pagano and Ricci's funeral ceremony was underway in Casablanca, the AISI began a sweeping series of raids, thanks to the information provided by Pagano. They arrested a score of corrupt government officials along with the four remaining members of the commission.

Alerted to the Mafia's illegal smuggling routes, the Italian navy deployed helicopters, aircraft, and surface vessels to intercept the smugglers. The drugs that were confiscated filled several large warehouses. However, the most gratifying interdictions were those that led to the rescue of nearly 1,000 souls who were being trafficked.

While the navy was making life miserable for smugglers, the financial crimes unit kicked off their day by confiscating the records and computers of bankers who were laundering the organization's money and moving their cash across international borders. They seized the banker's corporate, personal, and family assets, freezing them until they could prove to the government that they legally received the money that flowed into their bank accounts and paid taxes on this income. None could.

Pia Lamberti's black Range Rover HSE, with Zunino at the wheel, approached the Campo Verano, an early 19th-century cemetery near the Basilica of San Lorenzo fuori le mura. Several car lengths ahead of them was a hearse carrying the body of Carolina Biagi. Villa, Acardi, and the trio followed in the Defender.

Zunino, Villa, Bruno, and Donati removed the casket from the hearse and acted as pallbearers. Lamberti, Acardi, and Donais led the procession, stopping at a beautiful black granite tombstone in which, above Carolina's name, was a carving of the ring Lamberti gave her.

The service was brief. Lamberti said a few words, after which she placed a bouquet of red roses on the casket. Inside was a small stainless-steel box that contained the antique red agate cameo sterling ring. Once the ceremony was complete, Lamberti asked Acardi to accompany her in the Range Rover. They sat in the back.

"How is your arm?"

"The doctor will look at it next week. If I'm healing well, the sling comes off. If not, I could wear it for another four weeks. It's a pain in the ass."

"Let's hope it comes off soon. I asked you here because there's something I need to discuss."

Acardi sat up straighter, continuing to look at Lamberti, who was to his left.

"Tomorrow, the president will appoint you the director of the AISI."

Acardi's eyes widened in surprise. "There are dozens of law enforcement officials with more seniority than me."

"It's done. I either know or have researched the 31 who have more seniority. They're bureaucrats who have adequate leadership abilities but are incapable of running the fast-moving organization into which the AISI needs to evolve. Protecting world leaders from terrorists on our soil and shutting down the illegal activities of the largest bank in Italy are examples of what you've accomplished. Although you received little to no intel from government agencies, you brought those responsible to justice, although not necessarily through the judicial system. The AISI needs this type of leadership."

"There isn't much you don't know."

"Let's hope not."

"Credit Bruno, Donati, and Donais as being the major contributors to those successes."

"You're the catalyst. I want the four of you to work together. You're too good of a team to break up."

"They'll never agree to work for the government again. They like the freedom of being self-employed and selecting their clients, although I admit I haven't given them much choice in that regard. Also, Donais is a French citizen who is here on a work visa. By law, every so often, she has to leave the country and return to France."

"An easy fix. She'll be an Italian citizen by the end of the week. Since she's obviously not married to someone with citizenship and probably doesn't qualify by descent, I'll have President Orsini waive the current requirements and approve the request based on national security. My staff will draw up the paperwork, she'll sign it, and citizenship papers and a passport will be issued - as long as she and her associates agree to work with us."

"That's not enough to entice them back into the arms of the government. We'll need a sweetener or two."

"Such as?"

He told her.

"That's a decision for the new director of the AISI, not me. If you run into any barriers, mention you have my support. That should clear the way."

"If we go down this road, understand that they're not linear investigators and don't adhere to the letter of the law in solving a case."

"There's legal and moral justice. I don't care which they dispense as long as they get results."

Upon returning to the residence, Lamberti invited everyone to her office, where she opened two bottles of Louis Roederer Cristal champagne. Zunino poured the golden liquid into the flutes he'd handed out. Lamberti announced Dante Acardi's appointment.

"Well-deserved," Bruno said, a sentiment echoed by Donati and Donais.

Lamberti put down her flute and looked at Bruno.

"What case will the three of you work on next?" she asked, giving Acardi an opening to discuss their involvement with the AISI.

"At the moment, we don't have one because we don't have a client. I hope Dante will have something for us soon," Bruno confessed.

"Thanks to my new position, I may be able to provide BD&D Investigations with a steady stream of business," Acardi said.

"Why do I feel a caveat coming?" Bruno asked.

"A proposition. You can accept or reject whatever I show you. If you accept, I want priority on your time."

"As long as we can pick our cases and report only to you. Although that association has almost gotten us killed in the past," Bruno said.

Everyone laughed.

Donati and Donais agreed to Acardi's proposal.

"I'll need to work from Paris for part of the year because I have a work visa," Donais said. "There's nothing I can do about that."

"I can," Lamberti said, interjecting herself in the conversation.

"The only way to ensure that your work is unobstructed is to provide you with dual citizenship. Would you be willing to become an Italian citizen while still maintaining your French citizenship? I could make that happen within the week."

"Yes," Donais quickly responded.

"Then, we're all in agreement," Bruno said.

Lamberti raised her flute and, following the toast, asked everyone to have a seat. Zunino and Villa took their usual positions at the back of the office.

"Now that you've agreed to work with the AISI, perhaps I can suggest your first case. "Do any of you speak Russian?"

AUTHOR'S NOTES

This is a work of fiction, and the characters within are not meant to represent or implicate anyone in the actual world. That said, substantial portions of *The Mistress,* as stated below, are factual.

This novel is dedicated to the late Dr. Frank Sullivan, a close friend and former college English professor. This author's literary expertise was because of his tutelage, and any mistakes in writing should be attributed to the author's inattention to what he taught. In and beyond the classroom, a kinder soul never existed.

Trattoria alle lance is a cozy family-owned restaurant on a side street near the Santa Lucia train station, which the author came across when researching this novel. The restaurant's portions are large, the food excellent, and the wine pours generous. There is no semi-private alcove with a rectangular table nor a transition from commercial to residential properties on the street on which the restaurant is located. They were created for the sake of the storyline.

The author indicated that the Vigili Urbani issued security clearances to explain why Katarina Bruno would recognize the faces of the more nefarious persons within Italy. However, this isn't one of its functions. Instead, the Vigili Urbani is tasked with traffic control, local crime prevention and community policing, and administrative functions relating to licenses and urban regulations. They also serve as an auxiliary security police force. There are approximately 60,000 municipal police officers in Italy.

For the sake of the storyline, the author limited the number of Mafia families in Italy to five - to make discussions and the decision-making process among members easier. However, at one time, there were nearly 200 Mafia families in Sicily alone. The Mafia's governing body, the commission, exists - although it's unknown if there are formal meetings among members. It's reputed to have replaced the capo di tutti capi, or boss of all bosses, a Mafia title usually associated with a single individual who exercises absolute control within a defined area.

The Quirinal Palace in Rome is one of the three official residences of the president of the Italian Republic. The other two are the Villa Rosebery in Naples and the Tenuta di Castelporziano in Rome. At 1.1 million square feet and located atop the highest of the seven hills of Rome, it's one of the largest palaces in the world.

To the best of the author's knowledge, there are no ministry liaison offices in the Quirinal. These were placed within the presidential palace for the sake of the storyline as a convenient way to have Riva's mistress, along with those complicit in her death, at the Quirinal.

As far as the author knows, there is no escape tunnel in the president's office. This was created to get the bodies of Gratiano and Gabriele Riva into his office without detection.

The position of intelligence czar does not, as far as the author knows, exist. It was created to give Pia Lamberti tremendous autonomy and reporting only to the president.

The Ministry of Infrastructure and Transport was formed in 2001. Prior to that, the Ministry of Public Work and the Ministry of Transport carried out the responsibilities assigned to the present ministry. For the sake of the storyline, the author used the new ministry because of its influence in administering government contracts and took liberties with the description of Riva's office. Gratiano Riva is not a depiction of current or past ministers and that there is no implication that the Ministry of Infrastructure and Transport is or has been corrupted.

As represented, the Parioli area of Rome is in the northern portion of the city and close to the left bank of the Tiber and the Villa Borghese. The area was first developed in the 1930s and has a heavy concentration of the affluent and high society.

The EUR, or the Esposizione Universale Roma, is as represented. Private and public companies, and several government agencies, have their headquarters there. These include the Ministry of Health, the Ministry of Communications, the Ministry of the Environment, and Poste Italiane. Heritage Restorations is a fictitious company. The characters and other companies created by the author are not depictive or representative of any existing company or individual.

The description of the AISI, or Agenzia Informazioni e Sicurezza Interna, is as represented. According to *Intel Today*, it is responsible for safeguarding national security from threats originating within Italy's borders and protecting Italy's political, military, economic, scientific, and industrial interests. Information on the AISI can be found at: (https://gosint.wordpress.com/2017/05/08/introduction-to-italian-intelligence-agencies-part-iii-the-2007-legal-reform/).

My apologies to the Marriott Grand Hotel Flora. The author needed a large hotel near the Quirinal for the investigators to stay and meet with Acardi. This checked those boxes. On top of the Via Veneto, and next to the Villa Borghese gardens and the 2,000-year-old Roman walls, this neoclassical-styled Marriott is a beautiful place to relax when visiting Rome. For the sake of the storyline, Liberties were taken in describing the hotel's interior and parking, which is off site.

The effects of blast force trauma, such as that experienced by Dante Acardi, are accurately described. A more thorough explanation of what happens to the body when it's subject to an explosive force can be found at: (https://www.nationalgeographic.com/healing-soldiers/blast-force.html).

The Fate Bene Fratelli Hospital was established in 1585 and is run by the Brothers Hospitallers of Saint John of God. Liberties were taken with describing the hospital grounds and entrance.

As mentioned, ketamine takes three to four minutes to sedate someone. Hollywood makes it look instantaneous, but that's not the case. There is no antidote to reverse the effects of this drug. The only way to recover is to wait for it to wear off.

The information on Italy's Nucleo Operativo Centrale di Sicurezza (NOCS), which is part of the Polizia di Stato, is accurate. Their responsibilities include hostage rescue, recapturing targets from terrorists, and capturing anyone who intends to use force. As their deployment reaction times were unavailable, the author assumed that 30 minutes was reasonable. The type of aircraft they might employ was vague, and the author selected the CH-47, which is used by the Italian military and can carry up to 55 people. The NOCS weapons of choice for rifles include the MP5, MP7, Colt M4, and the H&K 416. For handguns, they usually carry a Beretta PX4 or a Glock 17. Photos of these weapons, along with other equipment and places described in the novel, can be found at alanrefkin.com.

There is no off-the-book detention center masquerading as the Ministry of Economy and Finance's Department of the Treasury building. This was done for the sake of the storyline to place Pagano in a facility where heavy security would be expected, and the public wouldn't flag the building as a prison.

Using lasers to pick up conversations within a building by analyzing the micro-vibrations from interior sound waves impacting windows is a proven technology. In recent years this has expanded to an eavesdropping technique known as lamphone, which allows for the monitoring of conversations within a room by detecting the minuscule vibrations that sound creates on the surface of a light bulb. Researchers are perfecting the detection of oscillations from objects within a space, such as a bag of potato chips or a houseplant, and converting these into conversations. For further information on this evolving technology, Andy Greenberg has written an excellent article in *Wired* that can be found at: (https://www.wired.com/story/lamphone-light-bulb-vibration-spying/).

The description of waterboarding is accurate, producing a drowning sensation that is very intense and inflicts acute mental and physical stress. According to the article referenced: "Within moments, one feels the strong sensation to gag; they inhale fluids, bringing on the true sensation of drowning." Death can occur from a heart attack and drowning, assuming the inhaled water is not evacuated promptly. More information on waterboarding can be found at:

(https://www.ballisticmag.com/2019/03/26/waterboarding-torture-preparation/).

Rokid glasses exist. However, for the sake of the storyline their use was extended beyond their current healthcare, medical, and industrial applications. Further information on these remarkable glasses can be found at: (https://www.rokid.com/en/).

ACKNOWLEDGMENTS

Once again, my thanks to those mentioned below for their time, advice, and thoughts. Sometimes an author can't see the forest for the trees. For that purpose, my friends always seem to have a chainsaw.

To Kerry Refkin for your invaluable help in editing and suggesting plausible alternatives in resolving situations within the storyline. You keep me grounded.

To the group - Scott Cray, Dr. Charles and Aprille Pappas, Dr. John and Cindy Cancelliere, Shirley Goodburn, Carol Ogden Jones, Doug and Winnie Ballinger, Ed Houck, Cheryl Rinell, Mark Iwinski, Mike Calbot, and Dr. Meir Daller for continuing to be my sounding boards.

To Zhang Jingjie for her continued expert research. Thank you, Maria.

To Dr. Kevin Hunter and Rob Durst, close friends of the author for decades, for advice on integrating technology into the storyline.

To Clay Parker, Jim Bonaquist, and Greg Urbancic. Thank you for the extraordinary legal advice you continue to provide.

To Bill Wiltshire. Thanks again for your superb financial and accounting skills.

To our friends-Zoran Avramoski, Piotr Cretu, Neti Gaxholli, and Aleksandar Toporovski. Thanks for your insights.

ABOUT THE AUTHOR

Alan Refkin is the author of seven previous works of fiction, and the co-author of four business books on China, for which he received Editor's Choice Awards for *The Wild Wild East*, and for *Piercing the Great Wall of Corporate China*. The author and his wife Kerry live in southwest Florida, where he is currently working on his next Mauro Bruno novel. More information on the author, including his blogs and newsletters, can be obtained at *alanrefkin.com*.